HIS HORROR THE MAYOR

Retired English teacher Tirzzy Quizenberry discovers a body at an old abandoned house. In spite of having taught nearly everyone in town, Tirzzy doesn't recognize the young female victim. Still, she's immediately certain who the murderer is. The police are sceptical — but Tirzzy knows what she knows, and she's determined to know more. With the help of her next-door neighbor Velma, and Julian, a giant on a motorcycle, Tirzzy intends to prove that Mr. Mayor is, indeed, a horror. And then she finds another dead body — in her own kitchen . . .

Books by Carol Cail
in the Linford Mystery Library:

WHO WAS SYLVIA?

eks.

CAROL CAIL

HIS HORROR THE MAYOR

Complete and Unabridged

LINFORD
Leicester

First published in Great Britain

First Linford Edition
published 2020

*A catalogue record for this book is available
from the British Library.*

ISBN 978–1–4448–4445–0

Published by
Ulverscroft Limited
Anstey, Leicestershire

Set by Words & Graphics Ltd.
Anstey, Leicestershire
Printed and bound in Great Britain by
T. J. International Ltd., Padstow, Cornwall

This book is printed on acid-free paper

Dedication:

To Michelle — thanks for giving me grandchildren as special as you are.

Prologue

To whom it may concern: If you are read-
ing this, it may be because I've been murdered.
This manuscript will explain my side of it.

1

I spread my white handkerchief on the curb, set my white vinyl purse on top of it, hefted the brick doorstop I'd brought from home, and sidearmed it through the jewelry store window. For several moments, the only sound was glass raining on the pavement. Then there was no sound at all except the night wind skating along the badly lit sidewalk.

It was such a quiet, lovely moment after the cacophony of destruction, I almost forgot the next step. Part of the pleasure of the moment was my exaltation that here I was, seventy years old, and I'd still found something new to experience.

Stepping closer, my sensible Oxfords crunching glass, I peered into the gaping store front at the spotlighted display of watches and rings. The logical thing to do was take the most expensive item, but jewelers disclose prices only verbally, in undertaker tones, and I doubted that

Jerome August (Jewels and Other Fine Things) would, even if he were here beside me on the shadowy sidewalk, give his unbiased opinion on what to steal.

I could just scoop it all — watches, rings, and even that turquoise pendant that looked like a wad of aqua bubble gum on a dog leash — into the aforementioned handbag. But one piece was all I needed, and, having been raised to believe economy was next to godliness, I selected the cheapest-looking ladies' watch, one with the type of old-fashioned black band that always makes me think of stocking garters.

The watch was artfully coiled around a vegetable peeler, which I actually wanted more than the watch. The entire window was decorated with kitchen flotsam and jetsam, and a little white card was propped up in the front — Have a Carat or Two. Jerome must have hired someone new — his window usually displayed merchandise and blue velvet, period.

I grasped the watch between forefinger and thumb and gently shook it free of the peeler. Stowing the loot in a patch pocket of my navy rayon dress — the closest thing I own to a black turtleneck jumpsuit like professionals wear — I stepped back to wait.

It seemed as if I ought to be hearing sirens by now. Preble City has only two patrol cars; they're usually both parked by the police station, and that's just six blocks away. But nothing was happening. No audible alarms. No squealing tires. No bullhorns or warning shots. Nothing.

I doubted I'd forget this, but I hunted my spiral memo pad out of the other pocket and wrote, 'Nothing.'

A minute oozed by. Bored, I yielded to temptation, returned to the window, and added the vegetable peeler to my haul.

It was at least five minutes before the police car, lights milling but no siren warbling, arrived. I had just about decided to walk over to the station and complain about the service.

The single policeman sat with one foot out the door and said something unintelligible to his radio microphone before he strolled over to examine the broken window. He stood companionably beside me and folded a stick of Juicy Fruit gum into his mouth.

'Did you see anyone, ma'am?'

I'd had this boy in school some years ago. Messman? Mussleman? Still waters run deep, but in his case they slowed to a trickle.

'I'm the one you want,' I told him sternly. 'See?' I fished out the watch to dangle under his nose.

'Now Ms. Quizenberry,' he imitated my scolding tone. 'Why don't you just run along home. There's nothing for you here.'

'Oh-yes-there-is.' Marching past him, I reached into the window again, and scooped up a handful of rings.

'Hey! What the devil has got into you?' Mussman or whatever said, catching my arm and agitating it so that the rings dropped into his own freckled hand. 'You want me to run you in?'

'Yes,' I said.

He scratched his chin, which rasped like a hoe on dry soil. Then he went to the patrol car, reached through the window for the mike, and told whoever answered that he needed a guard till the jeweler came downtown and a matron to take a confused old lady home.

I picked up my pocketbook and the handkerchief and dusted them together like chalkboard erasers. 'I can get home by myself. Messner, do you recall O. Henry in my class?'

'Was he the tall kid who always wore a red shirt?'

'Good night, Officer,' I said, taking four steps toward home before remembering the peeler, still in my pocket. I was of a mind to keep the thing as payment for my inconvenience, but the only person that would have hurt was me when my conscience kicked in. Returning to Messner, I handed it over.

Then I put one finger in the air to signify a recollection and trod glass again to retrieve my brick from its blue velvet backstop.

'You can't take that. It's evidence,' my old pupil protested.

'This is mine, and you don't know evidence when she's staring you in the face,' I declared and stamped off into the night.

I would have stamped, that is, if my arthritis had allowed. Part of my anger was over being snubbed as a suspect and part of it was for my failure to instill in Messner a lasting appreciation for O. Henry.

Of course, *The Cop and the Anthem* wasn't completely applicable in this case, though the result — failure to get arrested — was certainly the same. O. Henry's homeless protagonist Soapy suffered from cold and hunger, whereas a warm, soft Ohio night surrounded me, while a perfectly lovely home with a bed and a well-stocked pantry waited three blocks away.

No, I had tried to get arrested simply for the experience of it. And all I'd experienced was frustration. Breathing honeysuckle-laden air, I lifted my feet higher than normal to avoid possible sidewalk upheavals.

Write what you know. That's what the Your Own Write Correspondence School advised. And I know nothing about crime except for the newspaper and TV. How can I be a mystery writer if everything is a mystery?

★   ★   ★

My mainspring was wound too tightly for sleep. I sat up in bed with the Your Own Write textbook ('a handsome blue buckram-bound study guide') and uncapped the YOW pen ('black ballpoint on one end and fine-tipped red marker on the other').

The course materials had come this morning. The congratulatory letter from 'your personal expert, Marvin Golden' misspelled my given name from Tirzah to Tirazl, which I hoped wasn't any indication of Mr. Golden's level of expertise. I skimmed the directions which said, in sum, 'There's no hurry writing anything except the installment checks.'

The textbook was a delight to the eye and hand, its pristine pages tight and crisp, the spine crackling when I first opened it. Having read the table of contents, I yielded to the temptation of jumping immediately to chapter eight, 'So You Want to Write a Mystery.' That's what had led to my brick-throwing escapade tonight.

Of course YOW didn't advocate going

out and breaking the law to gain experience. What they said was, 'Seize every opportunity to actually see, hear, touch, taste and smell what you are writing.'

I believe the cliché 'rushing off half-cocked' described my approach to the writing course so far. Now I hooked my reading glasses around my ears and began more sensibly, at the beginning, chapter/lesson one.

'Don't be afraid to expose yourself on paper. In your journal, let your creativity gallop free. Don't try to write well, just write — whatever comes to mind. Scribble as fast as you can, and don't stop to reread or edit. Shut your eyes and, in the dark, vomit words from the pit of your right brain.'

I'd been reaching for a handful of the pistachios I keep in the night table, but thought better of it. Moving the blank loose-leafed journal ('beautifully designed in the same blue buckram as your textbook') onto my lap, I snapped off the bedside lamp, and began to scribble as fast as I could.

Ten minutes later, by the red numbers

of my digital alarm clock, I turned on the light and looked at what I'd written.

Having failed to space down at the end of lines, I had overwritten the same spot of the paper into one long inky smear, like an oil slick marking my submerged ideas.

★   ★   ★

'Tirzzy, did you hear about the brouhaha at Jer August's last night?' Velma Newby asked me across the green bananas in the Tisket Tasket Market.

I had slept as soundly as if I'd had a clear conscience. In the garish light of day and the overhead fluorescents, I was feeling more than a bit ashamed of myself.

'The insurance will pay for the window,' I said, ostensibly preoccupied with finding a perfect skein of red grapes.

Velma and I are next-door neighbors, and she's a widow too, though for only two years compared to my virtually forever.

In spite of what I'd just said, I knew very well where the insurance company would get the money to pay for the window. My conscience tweaked me, again, for Jerome August's next premium increase.

Velma invaded my floor space to begin her own grape-gathering. 'Seems really strange that nothing was taken.'

She smelled as if she'd recently had a permanent.

'Your hair looks nice,' I said for diversion. It did look nice — the white, glistening curls like scalloped shells. Her tanned face reminded me of seashores too, the wrinkles like tide lines, with gulls' feet around her eyes.

My complexion is more like beige tissue paper, crumpled around the mouth. My naturally curly hair is stark white. I never have got used to looking like this, like my Grandma Emma. Inside, my mind feels the same as when I was a girl.

Velma moved on to the anemic tomatoes, sneered and kept walking. 'It was probably Butch Deem. He probably broke the window and then forgot why, like the time he tried to rob the First National and forgot to cut eye holes in the brown bag he put on his head.'

I laughed. 'Poor Butch. A living example

that a little knowledge is a dangerous thing.'

'So what did you do last night?' Velma zinged, making me pick up a pint of mushrooms I didn't need.

'Nothing. Why?'

'I was checking windows at about eleven and saw you coming up your driveway.'

'Jogging around the block, is all,' I said and then, 'Look at that pyramid of soda pop, will you. Imagine how many trips to the bathroom that represents!'

*　*　*

Like a black hole, the YOW book sucked me straight to it when I should have been mopping floors.

Suggested activities. 1. Raise your eyes and stare straight ahead of you. What one object first snares your attention? Describe it. Tell a story about it.'

Since I was sitting at the kitchen table, what I saw was that blasted carton of mushrooms I had failed to put into the refrigerator. Rules are rules, so I began to write.

Mushrooms make me think of death.

My younger sister and I grew up in the best of two worlds — in town, across the road from our grandparents' farm. Our family didn't feel poor, but that's because we were thrifty and wise. Our idea of luxury was a warm toilet seat.

Some of the items that people consider special these days, we took for granted. Fried chicken fresh from the hen house. Handmade quilts. Clean air and pure water.

Mushrooms.

We'd look for them in the early spring, in damp, shady places that smelled of sweet rot. Around tree stumps, under canopies of green weeds seething up through soil the color and texture of coffee grounds. Sometimes we would search to find nothing, yet five minutes later the same surface would be boiling with new mushrooms, each pale cap wearing a garnish of shiny black dirt.

They weren't the smooth, bland mushrooms that supermarkets sell today. Ruffled and ribbed and the color of antique lace, they tasted like fork-tender beef steak. If I were sentenced to die, I'd want a heaping *plate of fried mushrooms for my last meal.*

Mushrooms weren't James's last meal, but they were one of the last.

We dined at The Golden Lamb the night before a Chesapeake and Ohio train carried him off to World War II. We'd been married one week.

That's all I want to say about mushrooms.

I slapped down my pen and began flipping through my blue buckram textbook, looking for a more interesting assignment. So much for being methodical about the lessons.

'Chapter/lesson nine. Perhaps you would like to write horror. Think of the things that frighten you. List them. How could you work one or more of these into a short story?'

Number one, I'm afraid of forgetting to renew my driver's license before it runs out and having to take the test again.

Here I paused to get my billfold and recheck that precious square of plastic. It isn't that I drive a lot, it's just that I can if I want.

Number two, I'm afraid of oversleeping

on the morning a Garden Club meeting is scheduled at my house. Along the same line, I literally have nightmares of having to serve them a sit-down dinner when all I have on hand is one Cornish hen, two onions, and a can of pears.

Number three, I'm terrified of losing my eyesight so that I can't read. So, just in case Mother was right, I never try to read without good light and never run with anything sharp in my hand.

Number four, falling and not being able to get up.

I supposed none of these fears had short-story potential. Undoubtedly the correct answers were snakes, spiders, vampires, or sociopathic children.

Sighing at the probable failure of editors to see the real possibilities for horror in the routine lives of the elderly, I flipped to the next lesson.

'Perhaps your talent lies in writing short fillers or crossword puzzles.'

I immediately returned to lesson nine.

Ghosts. Everyone is interested in, a little afraid of, ghosts. It would be easy to research a ghost story because ghosts are everywhere, even in packages of grocery mushrooms.

I wouldn't have to break any windows or laws either.

Unless, of course, you count trespassing.

★   ★   ★

Driving after dark makes me uneasy, and walking through a strange dark house would probably make me uneasier yet, so although night is best for experiencing haunted houses, late afternoon would have to do. The burning sun sent smoky shadows across the highway as my white Buick hummed me north out of town. The wind through the open windows knotted my hair and filled my nose with alfalfa perfume. (Air conditioning just leaves me cold.)

It was only about two miles to Preble City's token haunted house. The Linebarger place, a salmon brick four-square, had once been graced with beautiful gardens, fine furnishings, a happy family, and enough servants to keep it all that way. But too much to drink here, an indiscretion there, a great depression everywhere, and the mansion's glory days ended. It suffered a series of owners, each less desirable than the last. The grounds were allowed to run wild. The porches broke out in old furniture and appliances. The roof slowly caved in on itself like a face without teeth.

The final residents, before the house went perpetually empty, were a group of hairy youngsters of indeterminate sex, who kept goats and raised sunflowers and tried to hold up the Main Street Superbonanza with guns carved out of homemade soap.

After that, the house lay fallow, always for sale and never sold. Windows x-ed with boards, it deteriorated into the blight that children double-dared their friends to visit on Halloween.

Descriptions of a resident ghost varied widely. There existed no spectacular tragedy in the house's history to provide guidelines and substance for a truly satisfactory haunting. The most likely restless spirit candidate was Grandma Alice Linebarger, who'd been experimenting with a new tomato juice recipe when her pressure cooker exploded. Supposedly, on the night of a full moon, one can smell oregano a mile away.

Turning into the corduroy lane, I jounced its fifty-yard length and parked in the shade of a wild-limbed sycamore. When I shut off the motor, the silence rang in my ears. Gradually the birds and crickets and breeze resumed. I tucked my purse into my armpit and strolled toward the shade-dappled house.

The stone steps had crumbled around the edges, and the iron handrail shuddered to my touch. The buckling porch wheezed when I stepped on it. Imagining the planks snapping and swallowing my legs, I felt a little flutter of pleasure that my horror research was working already.

Cupping hands around eyes, I peered between the boards nailed across one of the windows at an empty room as gray and gritty as an old-time movie. Cool air breathed out of it, smelling of animal decay.

Testing the board barrier with a white-gloved hand, I sensed no hope of entrance this way. The other windows lining the porch wore the same, splintery armor, and the front door was shielded by a sheet of knothole-pimpled plywood.

I hadn't expected it to be easy. Holding to the flaky railing, I eased down the slab steps — one, left, right; two, left, right — and set out along an overgrown brick path into the side yard.

A bumblebee whizzed past my head on some emergency run. A mourning dove in the top of the ragged trees ho-oo- lia-ha-whoed monotonously. On both sides of the path, rampant poison ivy, glossy green, beckoned like wet paint to be touched.

I passed the slope of a gray weather-swollen cellar door that was almost submerged in a sea of tiger lilies. Turning the corner of the house, I surveyed the long back porch, a twin to the front, identical right down to the barricaded windows and plywood-covered door. I didn't even bother to haul myself up the narrow rock steps.

While I picked my way around to the other side of the house, I felt the first intimations of discouragement. I wasn't going to get in. If I sat in the Buick tonight, parked as close to the house as possible, would the experience be the same?

This side of the house, a southern exposure once terraced and fountained and gazeboed, lay in spectacular disrepair. The once elegant French doors cowered behind inelegant tar paper reinforced with chicken wire. I kept walking, toying with the idea of The Porch That Ate Preble City, and came full circle to the front again.

Hitching the purse higher under my arm, I considered. I hadn't brought any tools along, primarily because I'd been counting on previous trespassers to have opened the way for me. Now I was torn between being proud of everyone's responsible behavior and being annoyed at it.

The dove continued to sound as if he were blowing into an empty bottle. I toured into that side yard again and, stopping at the wooden cellar door, gave it a tentative push with one toe. The door grunted and puffed out dank, foul air.

Laying pocketbook-flat in a poison-ivy-free spot, I hooked my gloved forefinger through the rust-encrusted ring at the right edge of the door, screwed my shoes tighter into the ground, and heaved up-wards.

The door, lighter than I'd expected, whipped open and crashed sideways into the lilies, sending an unseen robin into hysterics. When it was quiet again and my eyes had adjusted to the gloom of the stairwell, I almost went into hysterics myself. A young woman lay on the top step, staring up at me without much interest.

Once the initial shock wore off, I stopped clutching my bosom and leaned to get a better look.

The woman was unquestionably dead. She hadn't blinked, for one thing, and, for another, her T-shirt and jeans were covered with a stain like melted pennies.

I mentally sorted through roll books, trying to place this face and give her a name, to no avail. All I knew about her was what I could see. She'd been a tiny little thing or she wouldn't have fit on the step, not even with her knees drawn up. Probably pretty. In her two hands, folded across her ruined chest, a single tiger lily also lay dead.

Trying not to feel too thrilled about it, I acknowledged to myself that this was murder. I might not know the poor victim. But by God, I knew who'd done the killing.

2

'Jerry Joe Hoffsteder?'

I nodded.

'His Honor the Mayor, Jerry Joe Hoffsteder?'

I continued to nod.

Police detective Paul McMorris arose from his squeaky oak chair and quietly shut the hall door.

I'd been treated like royalty ever since the police escorted me to the station for questioning. It was ma'am this and ma'am that and have some more coffee, every five minutes. Very different, I should imagine, from the attitude they would have taken last night if I could have convinced Officer Messman to arrest me for attempted theft.

They even offered to take my statement in the comfort of my own home. Eager to see the inner sanctum of a real — if wanting — police department, I insisted on being interviewed here, but it had been a disappointment. No uniformed persons bustling about, no phones ringing off the walls, no intercoms crackling, no guns or cages or glaring lights. Detective McMorris's office could have been my school principal's, except there wasn't enough paperwork lying around.

Resting one hip on the edge of his desk, he bent toward me. 'What makes you think Jerry Joe Hoffsteder murdered that woman?'

'I had him in seventh grade homeroom. Must be fifteen years ago. And, of course, in all his English classes through high school graduation.' I wriggled straighter in the extremely hard chair. It was surely one they used to wring confessions from suspects.

'And he struck you as the student most likely to commit murder?' Paul McMorris's eyes were the luminous gray of a summer sky after a rain. His white cumulus-cloud hair reinforced the image.

'I don't believe I ever had you in a class,' I said, knowing I never did.

He tipped back to laugh, revealing one gold tooth, upper left rear. 'You were a student yourself when I was in school. I'm Kenwood High, class of '42.'

I squirmed straighter yet and resisted a silly impulse to prod the curls on the nape of my neck. 'I don't recall seeing you around town before.'

'I haven't been here long. Retired from the Cincinnati Police Department a year ago, but retirement's too tame for me. Came here and talked them into letting me work part-time for minimum wage.'

I gave a ladylike snort of amusement. 'I'll bet your wife didn't like that.'

'She gave up on me a long time ago. We're divorced.' He folded his arms and crossed his ankles. 'But murder is what we're discussing at the moment.'

'Did you ever hear of O. Henry?' I asked, testing.

'You mean the candy bar?'

I could feel the muscles in my face sag.

'Or,' he went on, ''The Gift of the Magi' O. Henry?'

One of the few advantages to being old is you don't have to waste time on smooth conversational transitions. I'd learned what I wanted to know about

Paul McMorris, so I backed up to take a run at a previous topic.

'Our horror the mayor murdered the young lady,' I said.

'Why?'

'Why did he do it?'

The inspector shook his head. 'Why do you think that he would do such a thing? He's a respected, hard-working gentleman in this community. He's a shoo-in for re-election in the fall, and he's marrying May Ruth Brock in a few weeks.'

'Exactly. That's exactly why he killed that young woman. *An American Tragedy.*'

'Theodore Dreiser's novel.'

I couldn't help it. I beamed at him. Mr. M. was turning out to be a delight. 'Yes. Like the young social climber in that book, Jerry Joe foolishly involved himself with a young woman he now finds an embarrassment. Like his literary counterpart, he decides on murder to extricate himself. And like that other young man, Jerry Joe is going to suffer for his bad behavior.'

'So you saw, somewhere, sometime, our

mayor in the company of the dead woman?'

'I can see it right now,' I said, holding up both spread hands the way photographers do, looking between them at the imaginary scene. 'Jerry Joe says to Ms. X, 'Let's go look at this old house in the country that I'm thinking of buying. It needs a lot of work, but it could be a beautiful home for you and me and the children.''

'Children?'

'Future children.'

'But you didn't actually witness this conversation?'

'I didn't have to.'

Mr. M. sighed and eyed me as if he'd just caught me driving thirty miles per hour in a school zone. 'You're only guessing that he lured her to the old house and killed her. You have no evidence of it.'

'Oh, but I do. It's how I knew, as soon as I saw that poor girl, that Jerry Joe had killed her.'

'And what was it that tipped you off?'

I was sorry to hear his voice slip from friendly to disappointed resignation. It sounded like my own tone, whenever students claimed that their baby brothers had fed their homework to the family dog and thrown the crumbs into the fire.

'As I said, I had Jerry Joe in his seventh grade homeroom. We had a hamster that the children took turns carrying home over the weekends. When it was Jerry Joe's turn, he came back Monday with a shoebox wrapped round and round with cellophane tape and string, and he said the hamster — Fuzzy, its name was — had died in its sleep. During lunch period, the class held a funeral and buried Fuzzy, box and all, in a corner of the commons.'

Mr. M. gazed at me attentively, apparently hopeful that I was coming to a relevant point.

'Before that ceremony, however, my curiosity led me to take the shoebox to the teachers' lounge and remove all the fastenings. I was suspicious that the box might be full of wadded newspapers or something — that Jerry Joe had decided to keep the pet for himself. Jerry Joe's favorite charity was Jerry Joe. He perfected what nowadays is known as a Teflon personality. He could charm his friends and most of his teachers into believing that what was good for Jerry Joe was good for the school, the city, and the United States of America. But Fuzzy was in the box, all right. Well, not all right. Obviously his little neck was broken.'

'And you think Jerry Joe dispatched Fuzzy and therefore Jerry Joe murdered our young woman?' Mr. M.'s voice had gone from disappointed to out and out disgusted.

'No, no. Fuzzy's death could well have been accidental. But Jerry Joe had obviously seen dead people or cartoons of dead people. Because Fuzzy's little paws were rubber-banded together to hold in place — ' Here I leaned forward under the weight of each significant word. ' — one wilted lemon lily.'

Mr. M. exhaled the breath he'd been storing. He didn't laugh, frown, or otherwise disparage the story. Walking with his head bent in thought, he circled the desk and squealed his chair, settling in and back. He reminded me now of my

30

first principal, Mr. Wickworth, whenever I brought him some outrageous request, such as for a new stapler.

'It's all hearsay and circumstantial and insufficient,' he said.

'Do you need another bad character reference? How about the time I arrived one morning to find Jerry Joe and his best friend Stan Wright passing a waste-can back and forth outside two adjacent windows? They'd stuffed Sammy Brown into the can, his arms and legs poking out like sticks. Sammy was our token black student. Homeroom was two floors up, above the asphalt parking lot.'

'Terrible behavior. I'll never look at the mayor quite the same in future. But your story isn't relevant to the girl's murder. Unless we find something more tangible implicating Jerry Joe, there's nothing I can do.'

Now it was my turn to look disgusted.

'And Mrs. Quizenberry, I hope I don't need to advise you to keep all these unusual speculations to yourself. You don't want to find yourself being sued for libel.'

Studiously ignoring the pink that I could feel prickling my face, McMorris flipped open a manila file folder on his desk blotter. It held one sheet of paper that was one sixth full of typed lines. His case, so far, was definitely insubstantial.

'I'm not a blabbermouth,' I apprised him. 'I'm aware the police will want to keep the clue of the lily a secret so that when Je — the murderer is questioned, you can trick him into mentioning it and incriminating himself.'

'Well, it's certainly a possibility,' McMorris said, smiling at something amusing. 'There are one or two other details of the crime that would be better for that, though.'

I couldn't help trying to think what they could be.

'Number of shots,' McMorris said without looking up. Sighing, he shut the folder. 'When we know the young woman's identity, we'll probably know who killed her. It's fortunate you were wearing gloves. Perhaps we'll get lucky with fingerprints.'

I stood up, chin first. 'I certainly hope luck is with you since common sense seems out of the question.'

'Now, Mrs. — Tirzah.' He stood, too, and backed out of my path all the way to the door. 'Don't be angry with me. I'll keep your information in mind. But there really isn't anything more I can do about it.'

Well, there was something I could do.

At six o'clock that evening, when most people would be sitting down to supper, I telephoned Jerry Joe at his house and complained about the pothole in front of my house.

'Why, certainly I'll tell the maintenance department to get on it,' Jerry Joe promised. 'Tomorrow. When you could have reached them yourself. Nice to hear from you, Ms. Quizenberry.'

$$\star \quad \star \quad \star$$

I was preparing my own turkey on whole wheat when Velma knocked at the screen door and opened it. 'I want to hear every lurid detail,' she announced, helping herself to a sliver of white meat before sitting at the table.

'I'm sure the gossip must be more lurid

than the real experience,' I said, pouring her a cup of coffee and mining it with the two tablespoons of sugar she requires. 'I just happened to open the cellar door and there she was. Or wasn't, if you want to look at it like that.'

'First of all, why were you out at the Line-whatsit place anyway?'

I hadn't told anyone about investing $395 in a writing correspondence course. When the police asked me the same question, I said I was mushrooming. I couldn't tell Velma that and get away with it — she knows when mushrooms can be found.

'I was blackberrying.'

'Blackberrying this month! No, Tirzzy, what were you really doing out there?'

'I was looking for ghosts.'

'Oh, all right, don't tell me. Just tell me what you found and how you felt.' Velma folded her lips in on a swallow of coffee and sat back expectantly.

'I found this poor dead woman with blood on her front, and I felt as if I'd mis-stepped on a flight of stairs and had grabbed the banister just in time.'

'How long had the body been a body? Did it, you know, smell?'

I set my sandwich aside to try again later. 'No worse than Bea Adair when she comes to Garden Club directly from the gym.'

Bea is the oldest exerciser at the Y aerobics class. She looks like a Kewpie doll on steroids.

'You got any cookies?' Velma asked, rooting through my YOW materials on the table, obviously not interested in anything inedible.

'No. Velma, do you know Jerry Joe Hoffsteder?'

'Just to nod at on the street. His brother John Junior graduated high school same year as Marcia.'

Marcia, Velma's daughter, now lived in California with her second husband, two children, two stepchildren, second mortgage and, undoubtedly, second thoughts.

'Oh, yes, John Junior. I'd forgotten about him. Where is he now, do you suppose?'

'Last I knew, he bought a farm in Darke County and was raising tofu.'

I had a vision of pasty white stalks mushing down under a good rain. 'Soybeans.'

'Soybeans.' Velma twisted around on her chair and squinted at the empty kitchen counters. 'No crackers either?'

I rose to get her some pork rinds from the pantry. 'I always thought that whole family was on the weird side. John Senior is the meanest-looking veterinarian I ever did see — eyes like two BBs held in forceps eyebrows. And the mother, Cynthia, so flighty you want to tie her ankle to the nearest chair.' I picked up a pork rind and idly nibbled. 'Jerry Joe kept them in the closet during his last campaign. His little sister, too. Rosetta. Rosie the Razor.'

'What?' Velma laughed, spraying her front with fine crumbs. 'I never heard her called that.'

'Had a tongue like a stiletto. Still does, as far as I know. No tact. No cream of human kindness. No — you can imagine — friends.'

'So the whole family is a washout. What made you think of them?'

'Murder,' I said, licking my fingers clean.

After Velma went home, I opened the YOW text at random and read.

'Interviewing someone interesting in your community could be the start of your writing career. Chances are, the person who interests you would interest readers as well. Think. Whom would you like to know more about?'

Putting down the book, I went straight to the telephone and dialed the home number he'd given me earlier that day.

'Paul McMorris.'

'I'm in charge of the Garden Club newsletter, and I want to do an interview of you.'

'Mrs. Quizenberry?' he guessed. 'How did you know that I'm a gardener?'

'I didn't. That makes it even better.'

'How about tomorrow evening? Dinner?'

'My place or yours?' I'd always wanted to say that.

'I'll make reservations at the Heritage House for seven o'clock. Shall I pick you up?'

'No, thank you.' He already had.

★ ★ ★

Of course, I knew I couldn't send a handwritten assignment to my YOW writing instructor. I'd been putting off retrieving my college Remington manual from the basement, but now that I had happy thoughts to keep me company on the errand, I switched on the light at the top of the flight and carefully lowered myself into the depths. The dank, familiar smell rose up to meet me — a mixture of dirt floor, empty coal bin, gas furnace, concrete walls, and mold.

It's foolish to be afraid of a cellar. I wasn't afraid — the correct adjective would be squeamish. The stairs were steep and poorly lit; the space below was hard and cold; and everything was gritty and grimy and grim. Having lived here for thirty-some years, I had to admit that all of the drawbacks were my own fault. I could have built a rumpus room down there with carpeting, florescent lighting, and pictures on the walls. Or at the very least, I could have swept the steps every few years. However, it's been easiest to store things in the spare bed-room and venture to the basement only in the company of furnace repairmen and plumbers.

I had, however, unthinkingly stashed my typewriter down here years ago, when I was still spry. I found it in cobwebs under a stationary tub. By lifting it ahead of me up the steps and resting three times on the trip, I brought it into the blessed light of the hallway. The brown plaid case looked good as new, not counting the mildew stains and the hole in one corner where a mouse had teethed on it.

Spreading newspapers on the kitchen table, I hefted the case up to look inside. The typewriter still smelled of ink and oil. After the cardboard flakes, greasy dust and mouse droppings were brushed out, it should work fine. I would take it to the office supply store and have it tuned up. One day soon.

Meantime, I stowed it in the guest bedroom closet.

★   ★   ★

I went to bed before ten o'clock, setting my alarm. When it went off three hours later, I moaned, sat up, and reached to bring the extension phone closer. Dialing, I resisted the impulse to clear my throat, knowing a little mucous would add to the old-lady quaver.

'Mn-lo.'

'Jerry Joe? This is Tirzzy Quizenberry,' I dithered. 'Has the police department identified that butchered, unfortunate woman yet?'

There was a long, rustling silence. I imagined him raising up on one elbow to look at the clock. 'No'm. Not yet,' he groaned into the receiver.

'I'm having a terrible time getting to sleep tonight. I just can't get that awful picture out of my mind. That sweet face and all the horrible blood leaking out of her helpless body.'

'Take a pill. Or four.'

'Is that what you do? When you have things on your consc — your mind? Like, did you see that poor, bleeding girl?'

'No, ma'am. I'm the mayor. I don't get called to crime scenes.'

'Oh, of course.' My imitation of ZaSu Pitts was beginning to annoy even me. 'You're very fortunate. You wouldn't want to see all that dripping, crimson, spewing — '

'Ms. Quizenberry, it's nice to hear from you, but I'm going to let you go now because it's my goodness almost one in the morning. Good night.'

I cradled the receiver and slept like a hound dog in a patch of sunlight.

★ ★ ★

'Setting is where and when your story takes place,' my textbook lectured. 'See if you can describe your hometown so that your reader will realize it with all of his senses and will also recognize how you feel about it.'

Preble City was founded in eighteen-something and named for some general. It grew out from the railroad toward the corn and alfalfa fields. There are almost seven thousand people living here today.

And some not living.

I can envision where she lies, because

Dewey Foley held an open house at the mortuary the year he added the chapel and computer wing on the back. The prep lab, as he called it, is white — floor, walls, ceiling — and as chilly as the freezer aisle at the Tisket Tasket. You feel as if you're standing inside a snow cloud.

The tables and sinks and desks and stools and even Dewey's ballpoint pen are stainless steel that reflects the overhead fluorescents like a gray lake reflects moonlight. You feel this urge to speak in whispers, not so much out of respect as out of embarrassment that your regular voice sounds so whiny echoing back to you.

It smells like a doctor's office and Dewey's Old Spit aftershave. You want a stick of gum to take away the antiseptic taste. You hug yourself so as not to touch anything, and it isn't the sterility of the room you're protecting so much as your own.

Fred Bittman joked that Dewey was going to see all of us naked someday, but we didn't laugh much. I've always been ashamed of my cellulite.

And there's no one yet to mourn the

murdered girl, to dignify her lying there in the cold.

Oh, dear, I'd certainly wandered off the assignment. I put aside my homework, promising myself and YOW Instructor Golden to go to the library and look up the history of Preble City.

★ ★ ★

But first things first, I walked down to city hall to have a few words with Jerry Joe Hoffsteder.

It was lovely out. Sky the color of cornflowers. High, filmy clouds, like a layer of veiling. The smell of cut grass and turned soil and someone cooking tomatoes. My sensible shoes thumped the pavement in time to 'You Are My Sunshine', revolving in my head.

City hall looks more like city warehouse, a square, squat, brown-brick one-story surrounded by a parking lot. Inside, a vestibule the size of a boxcar contains a reception counter and a glass directory to the train of offices beyond.

I didn't need to sign in because I knew

43

where I was going. The mayor's office is the choice southeast corner overlooking the Dairy King.

When I met people in the skimpy hallway, we had to turn sideways to pass. That can't be good for employee morale. The wood floors under the dirt-brown carpet creaked like an accordion. Voices ricocheted off the maze of walls.

Turning into the open doorway at the end of the gauntlet, I rested my white purse on the oak desk barring my forward progress and announced myself. The young woman on the other side was probably hired for her hall-navigating ability. If she were any thinner, she'd have been two-dimensional. Smiling cut her face in half.

'Is the mayor expecting you?' she said, alter checking his appointment book for the right answer.

'Look at Monday. Was I supposed to be here then? Quizenberry.'

Obediently, she whipped back a few pages. 'No, I don't see — '

'I just want a second of his time. To tell him thank you.'

'I'm afraid he's rather busy right now,' she said, and a swell of male laughter came through the closed door behind her. 'May I deliver the message for you?'

'Oh, please, couldn't I just have a moment? I walked all this way.' I braced one hand in the small of my back and smiled bravely.

Neither of us had to give in, because at that moment the inner office door swept open and Jerry Joe followed it. He stopped, recognizing me, and his expression cycled from tranquil to annoyed, to politically correct.

'Ahh, Ms. Quizenberry. Janice, do you have city council minutes from last week?'

Janice rummaged on her desk. 'Mr. Mayor, this lady wanted to thank you for something.'

He raised his eyebrows politely. Fortunately, he hadn't inherited his father's black pincer brows, but unfortunately he'd inherited his mother's invisibly fair ones. Blue eyes, a reverse widow's peak with bony, bare temples. Long, square jaw. Not too fat, not too thin, not just right — a garter roll of waist overhung his too-tight tan slacks.

Snatching the papers Janice had found, he turned away, booming, 'You don't have to thank me. It was my pleasure.'

The door between us snapped shut.

'Nice of you to come,' Janice dismissed me. She picked up a pencil that was thicker than any of her fingers and began to punch out the phone buttons with it.

'Just let me catch my breath,' I said, leaning on the desk.

'Wouldn't you care to sit down?' she offered, giving me that concerned look which says don't get sick till I'm out of hailing range.

'No, if I get down, I won't be able to get up again. I'll sort of staunch here a bit.' I lifted a hip onto the edge of her desk and tried to look comfortable.

'Dee-Dee,' she said into the phone, bending to consult a note pad. 'Have you got a req for the electric department's Q A?'

While she continued to speak governmentese, I focused on Jerry Joe's appointment book. Reading upside down, an old schoolteacher's trick, I was satisfied that nowhere

46

in his schedule did it say, 'Murder mistress.'

Straightening, I waved and smiled at Janice, marveling again that a woman that skinny could wear a skirt without suspenders, and went home.

Whatever Jerry Joe thought I was thanking him for, it wasn't repairing the pothole in front of my house. I recalled a TV news story about a man who put things into potholes — salad greens, yellow plastic ducks — and called them art. My crater in the street cried out for whole heads of lettuce, real mallards; a gilded frame.

I took a shortcut across the overlong grass of my front yard, past the windows of my extra bedroom and living room, and past the obligatory but never used front door on its little stone porch with the little hat of a roof. Visitors always came to the south-side kitchen door because that's where the driveway ended at the detached garage. My bedroom occupied the back corner of the house, and the bathroom stretched long and narrow between it and the kitchen, seeming narrower for the sleek washer and dryer I'd had installed beside the claw-footed cast-iron tub.

It all resembled a 'before' picture in *Better Homes and Gardens*, but it suited me like a glove, a stocking cap, and an old lace-up shoe.

I didn't have to dig out my key, because I hadn't locked the door.

3

I hummed as I drove to my appointment with Paul McMorris. It wasn't often that I made an appointment that might also be called a date.

The Heritage House parking lot was humming, too. Once inside, I surmised the restaurant was hosting a high school reunion. It looked like the class of about 1965. Men standing swaybacked, bellies proudly thrust out in front. Women whose perfect hairdos appeared carved rather than combed. Several of them nodded at me and chorused, 'Hello, Miss Quizenberry,' sounding like themselves decades ago, even down to getting the courtesy title wrong.

I waved airily and kept walking behind the hostess, Mary Jo Emory, whose ample hips swished from side to side like a washing machine. Down two steps, up seven, and we were in the dim, quiet, back dining room reserved for lovers and real-estate salespeople.

Paul McMorris lifted his backside from the booth cushion in a brief, awkward show of courtesy as I wriggled in on the other side of the table. Mary Jo swayed from foot to foot, waiting for a drink order.

'Which of us is the designated drinker?' I asked Mr. M.

He cackled. 'You can be. I'm a total tea-er.'

'Make it two,' I told Mary Jo, relieved that I didn't have to pretend to like orange juice adulterated into carpe tools.

He was wearing a yellow tie on a yellow dress shirt under a gray suit jacket. I was wearing a gray dress with yellow beads and earrings. It embarrassed me, as if I'd done it on purpose.

'So, did you have a productive day?' I asked. 'Did you find out that poor girl's identity?'

'I thought we were going to talk about fruits and vegetables,' he said, shaking out his napkin and spreading it on his knees.

'That will take only a minute. Let's talk shop first.'

He reached across and opened my menu

as if I were handicapped. 'The specials are Swiss steak or chicken-fried pork cutlets.'

I shut the menu and set both elbows on it. 'What's her name?'

'Lisa Norvell. From Cincinnati,' he added before I could sort through memory for the name. 'Her brother confirmed the identification this afternoon.'

'What was the cause of death?'

'Gunshot at close range. Chest.' A couple whom Mr. M. apparently knew came into the room, and he smiled at them as he said this, as if it were some casual pleasantry.

Mary Jo brought the iced tea and took our order of two Swiss steaks. Violin music wafted from the overhead speakers: *From Here to Eternity*.

Now that the victim had a name and a brother, I felt better. No one wants to die unnoticed.

'Detective McMorris — ' I said.

'Paul.'

'Paul. Was she sexually molested?'

'No.'

'Has the medical examiner determined when she died?'

'Monday night. Probably between ten and midnight.'

I squirmed. My alibi, should I need it, was minding my own business throwing bricks through jewelry-store windows.

'Was the gun found?'

'Not yet.'

'Can you get a warrant to search for it at Je — ' Paul snapped up a warning hand and I changed it to 'you-know-who's house?'

'No, and I really do insist we change the subject to something more pleasant, like tomato worms and dry rot.'

'Where do you live that you can have a garden?' I obliged, picturing him in a three-room third-floor apartment in one of the old Victorians on First Street.

'I'll show you after dinner,' he said, eyes crinkling. 'You can come up and see my edgings.'

⋆ ⋆ ⋆

He lived in the entire house, a brick bungalow across the street from the high school. We looked at the back yard first, while there was still light. His vegetable garden was the picture of health, all rows straight and weeded and full of feathery green shoots. Along the property boundary fences, the first rank of flowering annuals were blooming — petunias and geraniums mostly — against a green backdrop of euonymus, pyracantha, and japonica. Nothing fancy, just good old meat and potatoes landscaping.

We strolled around to the front. The generous porch was festooned with hanging begonias, a rope hammock, and a porch swing with a yellow gingham cushion. I homed in on the swing, which jingled familiarly as I sat down. 'Now this is the life.' Folding my hands over my Swiss steak supper, I toed and heeled, back and forth.

Paul sat sidesaddle on the porch rail — a brick and cement wall, actually — and asked if I minded if he smoked a cigar. Cigar smoke reminds me of Dad, so my contentment spiraled another level.

'How long have you been interested in gardening?' I felt duty-clamped to inquire.

'It's relatively new for me. Last year

was the first time I enjoyed the vegetables of my labor.'

'A city boy, you said. Do you still have relatives in Cincy?'

'No. Nowhere.' In the fading light, his teeth flashed white to show he didn't mind. 'How about you?'

'My parents died twenty years ago. My sister Emma lives in Arizona. I didn't have children.' I couldn't smile about it, though I also couldn't cry.

The swing issued its obligatory squeak-squawk as I continued to glide. Lightning bugs blinked above the shrubbery. Once in a while, a car rushed past, usually leaking music.

The cigar glowed red and circled away and down. 'You going to ask me anything more about horticulture? Seems like it's going to be a pretty lightweight piece of writing.'

'What kind of plant would you be if you were a plant?' I wondered, feeling so mellow that even my knees didn't hurt.

'Hmm. An oak tree — long-lived and handsome and resistant to disease. How about you?'

'A water lily, floating on my back in the sun all day.' In the same idle tone, I added, 'What kind of plant would Jerry Joe Hoffsteder be?'

Paul didn't comment.

'A greater bladderwort,' I said.

'You stay away from him. Tirzzy, you hear me? I mean it.'

'I'll stay away,' I promised meekly.

Isn't that why telephones were invented?

★ ★ ★

'What is it now, Miss Quizenberry?' Jerry Joe mumbled into the receiver as my little digital alarm clock blinked over to 1:56 a.m.

'I was just wondering what your stand is on historical preservation.'

'Historical — '

'Preservation.'

'It's my wildest dream. Quizenberry, do you think you could restrict your calls to office hours from now on?'

'Oh, I hate to bother you when you're working. Have the police identified that young woman? Do they know who killed her yet?'

His mouth smacked, like he had a bad taste to work out. 'Why don't you phone Police Chief Kinabeck and ask him? Ask him about historical preservation too.'

'Oh, dear. You sound irritated. I'll bet I woke you. Here I am, wide awake, trying to forget the blood and — '

I was talking to an empty line. When I redialed, the busy signal bleated.

★   ★   ★

My plan for nailing His Horror did not depend upon my hounding him till he collapsed in a fit of confession. What I expected was he would try to murder me first.

Being, realistically, on the downhill side of my life and gathering speed, I wasn't too concerned about expiring in a good cause. There are days when I'd welcome the peace and quiet.

Thursday, when my joints all felt like rusty hinges, was one of them.

Sitting at my kitchen table, surrounded by YOW materials, I wrote out what I hoped no one would ever publish: *Whom it may concern: It's quite possible that Jerry Joe Hoffsteder will be responsible for my death soon. The reasons are: 1. Jerry Joe killed Lisa Norvell, 2. I know because of Fuzzy (ask Paul McMorris about this), 3. Jerry Joe knows I know.*

The telephone rang and I jumped like an unboxed Jack.

'What?' I said as soon as I could get to it.

'Ms. Quizenberry? This is Marvin Golden. How are you today?'

I stared at the refrigerator's random grouping of fruit and vegetable magnets, trying to get my bearings.

'Your Own Write instructor,' he prodded. 'Calling from New Hampshire.'

'Oh, uh-huh.' Had my first easy installment check gone astray? Had I forgotten to sign it?

'I just wanted to welcome you to the program and ask if you have any questions.' His voice was high and light. I pictured a young man in T-shirt and jeans, sneakered feet on cluttered desk, sipping from a can of pop.

'No. I understand it all perfectly.' I

shouldn't let my perception of him preju-
dice me. Anymore, everyone in authority
is younger than I.

'Good, good. I'm looking forward to
receiving your first assignment. Are you
working on something?'

'Yes, I am.'

'Good, good. Poetry? Fiction?'

'A true story.'

'Good, good. I look forward to
receiving it. You have a super terrific day.'

Gawd, Gawd.

★   ★   ★

I printed *To be opened in the event of
my death* on the number ten envelope
and drove downtown to put the accusa-
tion into my safety deposit box.

On my way out of the bank, passing the
line-up of tellers, I noticed a dark young
man waving his arms at Sue Garvey's
window. 'Do I look like a crook?' I
couldn't help overhearing him say, as
everyone else in a thirty-foot radius must
have also.

Actually, he did look rather criminous.

Lean and scowling. Prominent cheek-bones. Shaggy hair on end. Shiny black jacket held together by brass rivets and zippers — surely suffocating in this weather. Blue jeans with thready holes in both back pockets. Cowboy boots apparently made from gray alligators.

'Five lousy dollars to cash a paycheck?' he whined. 'What a dump-water town. You know why I'm here? To get my sister that somebody around here blew away, that's why. And you people don't have the decency to cash my bloody paycheck so I can take her body home?'

I drifted closer, and then plunged right in. 'Is there some way I can help, Mr. — uh — Norvell is it?'

He twitched around to glare at me. Sue tried to shoo me off, her eyebrows up to her hairline.

'You think you can get me some respect, be my guest,' the young man said.

Chief teller Mason Willard came up behind Sue either to give backup or keep her from running.

Smiling, I said, 'I could cash your check for you at no charge. Assuming it's not more than my little account.'

'Why would you want to do that?' His suspicion was rather flattering. Me, capable of con artistry?

'I'm a friend of Lisa's. I'd like to talk about her with you, over a cup of coffee at Café Klatch.'

I could see his avarice warring with his reluctance to spend time with a tiresome old biddy. Shrugging, he made up his mind. 'It's your dime.'

The paycheck that he endorsed — Leon Norvell — was from the Ohio Tool and Dye in the amount of three hundred seventy-nine dollars and seven cents. The paper was limp and slightly damp, from his sweating on it during the argument. I drew three hundred seventy-nine dollars from my checking account and dug a nickel and two pennies from my change purse. Then I signed the back of his check passed it over to Sue, who pounded it with her rubber stamp like she was tenderizing meat.

As she handed over my receipt, Mr. Norvell finished stuffing the bills into his scuffed brown wallet. 'Thank you, lady,' he said with real civility.

'Welcome. The name is Quizenberry. Mrs.'

We jaywalked over to the Café Klatch and I led him the last table next to the north window. I squinted out of the spotty pane while he took off his jacket and draped it on the back of the gimpy-legged chair. A fly lay belly-up on the sill, and I blew it off so it wouldn't remind Leon of his sister.

A young woman I didn't know wandered over to take our order. She had an order pad, two menus stuck under her arm, and a mouth full of gum.

'Just two coffees, please,' I said.

She wrote it down laboriously before strolling away.

'Did you live with your sister?' I asked, noticing that, close up and full face, Leon looked younger and cleaner.

He shook his head. 'I live with my girlfriend.'

'Please convey my sympathy to your parents.' He stared blankly, so I added, 'About Lisa.'

'I don't know where they are. They sort

of ran away from home when Lisa and I were old enough to take care of ourselves.'

I clucked and frowned. 'What did Lisa do for a living?'

'I thought you said you were friends.'

'People can be friendly without actually knowing other people well. Do you know what I mean?'

No, his expression said.

'Leon, I'm the one who found your sister's — your sister. And it made me so angry, I'm now trying to find her murderer.'

He shifted impatiently and threw an elbow over the back of the chair. 'That's what we pay the police for. Let them do it.'

'I wish they would. But they're completely disregarding some very pertinent information I gave them, so I feel I must make an effort to serve justice myself.'

'You think you know who did it?' His widened eyes took another five years off his appearance.

'I'm sure I do.'

He leaned toward me, knocking over the salt shaker. 'Who?'

'I can't tell you that. I have to prove it first.'

Leon lowered his voice another notch. 'You thinking of blackmail?'

'Heavens, no,' I huffed, though for a few seconds I did think about it. The money to go to charity, of course.

The waitress brought the coffee, spilled both cups in front of us, dug several creamers out of her apron pocket, and slouched off.

'Well, so what do you want to know?' Leon asked, picking up his cup and dabbing the underside with a napkin.

'Everything you can tell me about Lisa. Where she worked, what her interests were, whom she dated. She wasn't married?'

'Huh-uh. She lived with a couple guys. Not at the time, of course.'

'Names?'

'Uhh, Eric . . . ' He shut his eyes and popped them open. 'Hershey. And another guy, Rod something.'

'What do they look like?'

'Bikers. Big, burly, hairy — both of them. Tattoos and stuff.'

These two did not sound like the nice

bicycle-riding boys I used to know. I guess, like so many things, the sport has deteriorated. 'No one else?'

'Oh, probably. I didn't keep track of her.'

'Did you ever hear her mention someone named Jerry Joe?'

'Sure. Maybe. Not that I remember.'

Disappointed, I sank back and picked up my cup.

Leon jutted his jaw and stroked at his throat with the knuckles of one hand. 'I liked Lisa, but she wasn't what you'd call, you know, warm. She kept stuff pretty much to herself. Which was fine with me, because I didn't want to deal with her problems on top of my own. Money, for instance. She never bugged me for a loan or anything. I guess bartending pays better than it looks like it would.'

'She tended bar? Where?'

'Delvachio's. It's a yuppie restaurant, downtown Cincinnati.'

I scrabbled through my handbag to get my notebook. 'Can you tell me the names of any of her girlfriends?'

'She didn't have any.'

'Oh, surely — '

'She didn't. Men, she liked. Women, ehhh.' Here he shrugged to indicate Lisa's attitude. 'If you're planning to snoop around at Delvachio's, they can give you names of females she hung out with, but take my word, she didn't do it on a serious basis.'

'Give me her address and your phone number — just in case.'

He made a grasping motion, and I handed the open book and pen to him. He printed three lines of capital letters and passed the materials back. 'That's it, when she wasn't sleeping over with one of the guys.'

'So there were several boyfriends?' I fanned at my face with the notebook, ashamed that the dead Lisa appealed to me more than the real life one.

'No doubt.' It sounded like no duh. 'Who, I couldn't tell you.' Tilting the coffee cup, he chugged it down and pushed back his chair. 'Gotta go. Take it easy.'

'You also.' My mind churned, certain there must be something key I should ask before he disappeared. 'Are you taking Lisa home today?'

'Naw. We don't have a cemetery plot or anything. The undertaker's going to cremate, once the police say so. Which should be any day, what they told me.' He backed down the room, pointing alternate arms into jacket sleeves.

Just before he turned to stride away, he smiled his first smile at me, and another decade slipped from Leon's face. He was one of my seventh-graders anticipating the dismissal bell.

★　★　★

I didn't want to drive into Cincinnati by myself, so I invited Velma along.

'What do you want to go all the way to the city for a drink for? I've got some perfectly good Morgan David here,' she malaproped.

'You weren't listening,' I shouted patiently. We were standing in her little front vestibule where her toy Manchester terrier, Yappy, was living up to his name. 'I want to see where that unfortunate

66

young woman worked.'

'Shut up,' Velma said.

Assuming she meant Yappy, I continued, 'It'll be a nice summer field trip. Supper. Maybe a floor show.'

'Oh for goodness sake — you know Tirzzy,' she scolded the little black dog, whose act included dashing around us in toenail-clicking circles. 'You've known her for years.'

Reasoning with Yappy was like reasoning with a blender full of walnuts and no lid.

'I'll pick you up in an hour,' I screamed and let myself out.

The hour later, she got into my car and said, 'Explain this to me again?'

I looked both ways and backed into the street. 'I'm ninety-nine and forty-four one-hundredths percent sure I know who killed Lisa Norvell. Now I'm out to prove it.'

Velma had been struggling with her seat belt. She settled back and panted, 'Funny, you don't look like Miss Marble.'

'*Marple* is fiction. This is seriously real.'

'So who did it? Oh, look, The Style

Shop is having a sale on hosiery.'

'I can't tell you. I don't want to be sued for libel.'

'Oh, come on.'

'No, no. Besides, I don't want to endanger you. It isn't safe to know too much.'

'Oh, come on! You sound like a bad movie.'

I sniffed and watched my driving.

Velma rearranged her skirt and folded her hands. 'I would never tell anyone you told me. I'd be safe and so would you, as long as I cross my heart and hope to die.'

'Don't say 'Die'!' We'd cleared the city limits, and I increased our speed to forty. Paul McMorris hadn't said I couldn't discuss the murder, just that I shouldn't publicly accuse anyone of it. 'It would be a relief to talk it over with you.'

'Feel free.' She sawed her shoulders deeper into the seat and waited to be entertained.

And she did find it amusing.

'Jerry Joe? Jerry Joe?' Velma kept guffawing. Fuzzy made her laugh, as did my account of the crank phone calls designed to annoy Jerry Joe into a fatal admission.

'You want me to call him for you

tonight, Tirzzy? So you can get your beauty sleep?'

'You aren't going to let on that you know, remember?' I frowned across at her. Maybe Velma was finding this story too good to resist relaying to her other cronies. I began to wish it all safely back behind my closed mouth.

'Tirzzy,' she said, laying her soft, dry hand on my forearm, 'I won't breathe a word. I want to save it to sell to the *National Inquirer*.'

Darn and drat! Was Velma a closet freelance writer too?

4

Delvachio's was easy enough to find; a parking space wasn't.

By cruising the wrong way on a one-way alley, we located a tiny lot marked off with tiny spaces and one tiny sign reading 'Restaurant Parking Only.' Then we walked a block, back to the restaurant we wanted.

Delvachio's was not the kind of place I'd have picked to have a nice, quiet dinner. The moment we stepped through the entrance, voices, jazz, and the clanking of dishes and silverware assailed our ears. Cigarette smoke hung in the long, narrow room like swamp gas. The light bill must have been a joy to pay; it was mostly beer neons and candles in red goblets.

The hostess was promptly on the scene, running interference for us to a table the size of a chessboard. It occupied a raised platform overlooking the bar, at which casually dressed people double and triple parked.

When Velma opened her menu, it overlapped mine. 'Look at these prices. Maybe I'll just get a salad and coffee.'

'I'm buying. Get whatever you want. I'll write it off my income tax as a business expense.'

Velma snorted. 'You mean when you get your license to be a private eye?'

Actually I was thinking of it as a legitimate deduction for writing research but, still unwilling to expose my dream, I nodded and warped the menu toward the flickering candle light. When the waiter arrived — a tanned, compact young man with a smile like a TV preacher — I asked for a Coke and whether he'd known Lisa.

'Mmm, not very well. Did you?'

Ignoring his attitude, I ordered the fish basket. Taking me at my word, Velma asked for lobster. The young man strutted away, and a frightened-looking Oriental busboy rushed in to give us ice water.

'Thank you. Were you acquainted with Lisa Norvell?'

He shook his head. 'I don't know anything about the liquors,' he vowed and slipped away.

'Two strikes,' Velma said. 'I'd ask her.' She nodded at a waitress who'd stopped at the bar to pick up an assorted drinks order.

The woman, who was too tall for her short black skirt, hefted a tray the size of a manhole cover onto her shoulder and ferried it deftly to the waiting party of ten. An old pro.

'Excuse me, miss,' I waylaid her on her return trip. 'I'm trying to find someone here who knew Lisa Norvell.'

'What for?' She was poised to get on with her work, staring down her narrow nose at me as if she were wearing bifocals, which she wasn't.

'I'm a friend. I want to bring her killer to justice.'

'Honey, if you were a friend of Lisa Norvell's, I'm Vanilla Ice's fiancée.'

I didn't know Mr. Ice, but I got the general idea. 'Even though I wasn't acquainted with Lisa personally, I want to stop the killer before he kills again. Did you ever meet any of Lisa's gentlemen friends?'

The waitress leaned closer and I smelled gardenias. 'The word 'gentlemen' doesn't fit, but, yeah, I know Hershey and old Rod and George and Dave and — '

'How about Jerry Joe?' I certainly hoped that at least some of Lisa's friendships were platonic.

Someone hailed our informant from another table, and she held up a maroon-nailed forefinger in that direction. 'No Jerry Joes that I know of. What's he look like?'

Velma piped up, 'A young Dick Van Dyke with less hair and more stomach.' I'd been wondering where to get a photograph of Jerry Joe to show people; maybe it would be easier to find Dick's in an old *TV Guide*.

The waitress skewed her mouth sideways in an attitude of hard thinking. 'Yeah, come to think of it, I do remember a guy like that. Picked her up from work a time or two.'

I clasped my hands together against my chest, thrilled.

The patrons who were trying to get service called her again, and Velma twitched around and snarled at them.

Our fount of information began to back

away. 'His name wasn't Jerry Joe, though. Lisa called him Jay Jay.'

'Eureka!' I said, knocking my ice water into Velma's lap.

★ ★ ★

'It's only eight-thirty,' I said, my hand on the Buick's ignition. 'Let's see if we can find where Lisa lived.'

Velma belched gently into her fist. 'Dine me on lobster, I'll follow you anywhere.'

'There's a Cincinnati map in the glove compartment. I hope.' I switched on the interior light, and our laps and tummies superimposed their ghostly reflections on the urban landscape beyond the windshield.

Velma rooted out the map while I sorted my notebook from the depths of my pocketbook. I found the page where Leon Norvell had printed his sister's address.

'Broom Place. Is that in the index?'

The map and Velma wrestled briefly. 'Three-G. That's northeast.'

'Reading Road,' I said, and started the car.

We lost our way only once, and that was because we were following a pickup truck full of furniture and became so involved in verbally separating the antiques from the chaff, we missed our turn.

Broom Place proved to be the last cross street in Pleasant View Mobile Home Park. Lisa's cream and blue house trailer was the only one with all the doors and windows shut and lights off. The rest of the neighborhood was enjoying a hot summer night, sitting on patios, barbecuing hamburgers, walking dogs, playing kick-ball on a cul-de-sac. I nosed the Buick into the edge of Lisa's dandelion-infested yard. As soon as the motor shut off, we could hear the Reds playing baseball from a scattering of television sets.

I swung my legs outside and stood, squinting one way and the other. The mobile home on Lisa's left had a concrete patio under a green plastic canopy. The other side of Lisa's place was a double wide unit made triple by a screened porch. The whole line-up looked about as portable as a string of airplane hangars. In the flanking yards, a swarm of children, none taller than three feet, whooped it up.

Velma came around beside me. 'How about them?' she said, tipping her head at the mobile home directly across the street.

A man and woman sat slack-limbed in redwood chairs in front of the most impressive unit yet. It had gables, bay windows, and a columned front porch with flower boxes full of geraniums — a Victorian mobile home. The couple openly eyed us.

'Hello,' I called ahead, crossing the center peak of the sloping street. 'Nice evening.'

They didn't encourage us by answering. The woman wore a sundress the color of overripe watermelon, an unfortunate shade for her round figure. Ankles crossed, *Good Housekeeping Magazine* in her lap, she reminded me a little of my Great Aunt Edwina, who had never once smiled or cried in my presence.

The balding, overweight man, wearing a T-shirt stained with brown paint or possibly chocolate, shuffled his feet as if some vestigial instinctive courtesy urged him to stand. Without ever making it out of his chair, he subsided and said, 'Help you?'

'We're sorry to bother you, but we're looking for someone acquainted with Lisa Norvell, the young lady who lived across the street.' I seemed to be the only one who felt like smiling.

'She owe you money?' the man said. 'If she did, you're out of luck, 'cause she's dead.'

'Nothing like that. We're helping the police with their investigation. What we want to know is, who visited Lisa in the last six months or so?'

They both stared at me as if they'd asked the question and were interested to see how it would be answered.

Velma said, 'Any men who looked like Dick Van Dyke?'

'You're leading the witnesses,' I warned out the side of my mouth.

'Nope, I wouldn't say any looked like Dick. More like Jerry,' the man said.

'What?' I had to restrain myself from rushing over and grabbing his non-existent lapels. 'Jerry Joe?'

'Jerry Van Dyke,' he said. 'You know, the younger brother. A little heavier. Bigger nose.'

'This person spent some time here with Lisa? Very often?'

'Dunno. We seen him what?' He looked at his wife for coaching. 'Two, three times?' She nodded.

'What was he driving?'

'Her red Jeep.'

'Were they always on good terms? Did you ever hear them arguing?'

'Never,' the wife abruptly spoke up. Her voice was a husky bass that made me think of unfiltered cigarettes and whiskey without rocks. 'Lisa was a good neighbor. Quiet and polite.'

The mister nodded and nodded. 'She was nice and quiet. She was hardly ever home. We'll miss her.'

Coincidentally, one of the children in the neighboring yard began to yip like a stepped-on dog, and many other little throats took up the refrain.

I raised my own voice to ask, 'So you can't think why anyone would have wanted Ms. Norvell dead?'

'It was prob'ly drug-related,' the man said.

'Was Lisa involved in drugs?'

'Not that I know of. I meant some slum scum needed a fix and mugged her for the price.'

'Oh, uh-huh. Is that what you think, too, ma'am?' I smiled encouragement at the lady, but she was too busy watching her husband to see it.

'What he said,' she said. 'Drugs should never have been rented.'

'Well, thank you both,' I said, peering around at the adjoining yards, trying to decide whom to question next.

There were no mobile homes behind Lisa's; a chain-link fence divided the trailer park from an unkempt vacant lot.

I asked our reluctant hosts, 'Do you know which neighbor would have known Lisa best?'

'Us,' she said, as 'Nobody,' he said.

When I frowned at them, the man flapped one hand. 'Like we told you, she wasn't here much. Them people over there —' He dipped his head. ' — they been here a week. Over there, the Pattersons, they've been here a month. We been here five years.' He leaned forward to spit between his feet. 'It won't do you any good to talk to anyone else. A waste of your time.'

'Oh. All right. Thank you.'

I linked arms with Velma for the trek across the dim, uneven street. My feet wanted to veer us off to talk to the Pattersons, whose children were now singing 'Jingle Bells' in the key of scream. But how could I ignore the four eyes boring into my back, waiting for me to blatantly reject good advice? Velma and I reinserted ourselves into the Buick.

We drove home with the radio on, listening to the Reds outlast the Cards. Velma said it wasn't the same as seeing it on TV; she especially missed the crotch-adjustments.

* * *

At three the next morning, armed with the conviction that right makes might, I dialed Jerry Joe, intending to ask his opinion of the Reds' chances in this year's pennant race.

'The number that you have reached is no longer in service,' the recorded female voice droned.

Well, I haven't reached it then, have I?

The live operator would not disclose the new, unlisted, number.

Waiting till a decent hour the next day, I phoned Jerry Joe's fiancée, May Ruth Brock.

'This is your United telephone operator calling,' I said. 'We're running a contest, and your name and number have been selected.'

'Ooo! What do I have to do? I've never won a thing in my life. Oh, well, of course, I got to be cheerleader, and then I got homecoming queen when I was a senior. And once I won a free hamburger when I scratched it off the token at Dairy King. Oh, and once I almost won the lottery, except I was two numbers off. But never ever have I won — what did you say the prize is?'

I had stopped trying to ford this verbal stream of consciousness, and for a moment I forgot why I'd called. May Ruth didn't sound a day older or an hour smarter than when she teased her hair and the boys in first period English class.

'You haven't won anything yet,' I said. 'But if you give me the three telephone numbers you expect to call most often during the next month, you'll be automatically entered in the drawing for a trip to Chechnya.' Sorry. It's the first place that popped into my head.

'Ooo, well, let's see. There's my father, 534–9909.'

'Good.'

'And my mother, 534–2222.'

'Mm-hmm.'

'And either my fiancé or my hair stylist — gosh, which should I go with?'

'If you win, the telephone subscriber wins something too,' I ad-libbed.

'Oh, well, then make it Mr. LeRoy — 534–8765. Have to keep on the good side of the man who does your coiffeur.'

'Dear, since you had such a difficult time deciding, let me enter that fourth number for you also. It's bending the rules a bit, but you sound like such a nice young thing.'

And so I got Jerry Joe's brand new

unlisted number. I propped it against my bedside clock to be handy sometime much later.

Then, feeling clever and in charge, I opened my YOW text. Mr. Golden was, after all, eagerly waiting to see what I could do.

'Over forty-five percent of mass-market paperbacks sold every month is romance,' I read. 'Are you interested in romance?'

Well, of course I'm interested in romance. Just because my husband was killed in 1943 doesn't mean my desires were too. Just because I never married again doesn't mean I've given up eating and sleeping and whatever else comes naturally.

It's been hard, though, in a small town with its limited male inventory, finding a suitable suitor. The trouble was, James died before the gloss wore off, before I'd seen him sweaty and unshaven on a Sunday morning, reading the sports page in his underwear. I'd compare every man I encountered to the handsome, smart, witty, strong James who smelled of green grass and tasted like warm pretzels.

James and I met in first grade, assigned the same table because my maiden name was Quince. I've always been grateful that Miss Fangmeyer had no more imagination than to seat the class alphabetically. Isn't that the perfect name for a teacher! But she didn't fit it at all. She was so cheerful and kind and patient with us, once I slipped up and called her 'Mother', and was mortified by everyone's laughter.

Anyway, James and I were best buddies straight up through high school, when it became more complicated than friendship. I remember sitting in the front seat of his father's Chevy, out on Seven Mile Road by a sibilant cornfield, thinking that I could never wait for graduation to be married. Desperate for official blessing to what we were and how we felt. His soft sweet breath on my face.

We received our diplomas. Next, James's folks insisted he finish college before he could marry me. I'm ashamed to say that I never have forgiven them. While I waited for him to turn into a mechanical engineer, I earned a teaching degree. On the weekends we took long drives and touched *one another and talked and didn't talk.*

We were married in my parents' dim living room, where every horizontal surface held a homemade, home-grown bouquet. I felt special in a blue gabardine suit and a pink rose corsage, with a scrap of veiled hat pinned to my hair. James had to put his wedding band on his little finger because a mosquito bite had swelled the ring finger. His brother Clifford kissed me on the lips and it was the first time any other man had done that, and I thought it would be the last.

Oh, sugar! Here was something else I couldn't send to Marvin Golden. Pushing everything aside, I stood up to brew a cup of tea.

★ ★ ★

I may be brave and an idealist, but I'm not a fool. I put on my best blouse and walked down to the police station to give Paul McMorris one more chance to land Jerry Joe himself.

Paul was in the lobby when I pushed through the glass door. Seven little Cub

Scouts fidgeted around him while he talked and pointed at a city map on the wall. The den mother looked like Jenny Southworth, but it was probably her daughter or maybe even her granddaughter — time does seep away.

'Everything outside the blue lines is the sheriff's territory and responsibility,' Paul was saying as I joined the group.

'What if that dead lady had been lying right on the line, half on one side and half on the other?' a red-haired cherub postulated.

'Then the sheriff and we would get together and see who wanted to handle it.'

'Flip a coin, you mean?'

'Maybe that would work. Now if you'll follow me down this hall, I'll show you the holding cells.'

'Is there any crooks in them?' a hopeful voice queried.

I tagged along at the end of the line, one hand stirring my handbag for notebook and pen. We went through a gray metal door into what reminded me of my grandfather's old barn — a central open area surrounded by stalls. I pictured Jerry Joe sitting in that one there, on the summer camp cot, oversized chin in his hands, contemplating the cement floor and his sins.

The children's voices echoed around the room, shrill with skittish excitement. Paul's low, measured words were like a bass viol amidst the piccolos. 'You see, here is where we push the meal tray through the bars, so we don't have to dock the door.'

'It's awful skinny,' one of them noted. 'You got a stack of pancakes and, plop, the top ones scrape off.'

'Yeah, and then the bars are all sticky,' another piped. 'So if the guy grabs them, he's stuck and he's got to stand there.'

The cubbies continued to speculate while Paul and the den mother smiled indulgently. My own speculations were that Jerry Joe was going to hate it here, pancakes or not.

When the tour was over and the boys had shouted their thanks and surged out the front door, Paul took me to his office.

'Nice to see you, Tirzzy. What's on your

mind?' He waved me into a chair and settled into his own chirpy one.

'I've brought you new evidence via a neighbor couple, across the street from where Lisa lived. They said a man who looked like Jerry Joe was at her house several times. And a young lady who works where Lisa did — she recognized Jerry Joe's description, too. Only she knew him as Jay Jay. He picked Lisa up from work occasionally.'

The longer it took for Paul to say something, the more my hopes slid. He pulled at his lower lip, eyes fixed on a point above my head.

Finally, just as I was about to say, 'They're all impressive witnesses — the waitress knows Vanilla Ice,' Paul spoke up.

'I can't believe you, out there interrogating people.' He said 'interrogating' as if it were disgusting, instead of the very thing that he gets paid for. 'Did anyone see Jerry Joe argue with or strike Lisa? Did anyone see him in possession of a gun?'

'Maybe not, but — '

'There's no law says a man can't give a woman a lift after work. Just knowing her doesn't incriminate Jerry Joe.'

I sighed and struggled up. 'You need more, I'll have to get you more.'

'Tirzzy, I've told you and told you — '

'So don't tell me again.' I meant to flounce to the door, but the arthritis turned it into a spasmic shuffle. 'Why don't you come to dinner at my house about noon Sunday?' I surprised myself by asking.

'All right,' he snapped, as if I were nagging him to carry out the garbage.

★   ★   ★

At two-fifty a.m., I tried out Jerry Joe's new unlisted number. A rain had come up, one of those soft, steady summer showers that sounds like heaven and smells like earth. I dialed to the gurgle of the drainpipe beside my window, and distant thunder overlaid the first ring.

The receiver came off the hook and a moment's silence preceded Jerry Joe's wary, 'Hello?'

'Hello, Mr. Mayor. I don't know if you remember me — Tirzah Quizenberry?'

His roar of disbelief ached my eardrum.

89

'Quizenberry, what do you want from me? You are driving me crazy. If you don't stop harassing me, I'm going to — I'll — '

'What I want to know this time is this,' I said in the nice-but-firm way of a door-to-door salesperson. 'All this talk on the news about banks and savings and loans failing has me very concerned about my nest egg. I think tomorrow I'll go down to the bank and take it out and keep it here at the house. What do you think?'

'I'm going to hang up now. And then I'm going to disconnect the phone.'

'Of course, $50,000 is a lot of cash money to leave lying around the house,' I hurried on. 'Where do you think I should hide it?'

After five seconds of silence, he did hang up.

If my wishing could make it so, Jerry Joe would now be lying wide-eyed on his back, chewing on the bait.

The first thing next morning, not counting dressing and coffee, I intended to buy a gun. I might be reckless, but I wouldn't be defenseless.

5

I hadn't been inside the High Noon Firearm Emporium since when the building was a dentist's office, so I stopped a few feet past the door to look around. It was all old-fashioned glass cases, the kind that come up to an average person's breastbone, the better to see the shelves of handguns. The walls were glass-cased too, full of shotguns and rifles standing at attention. The room smelled like oil and metal and glass cleaner.

At the far end behind an old-fashioned cash register, a bearded man tilted his face down to peer at me over his reading glasses. 'Help you?' he wondered with the enthusiasm of a stranger expecting to be asked directions to somewhere else.

'I'd like to purchase a pistol,' I said, marching toward him. 'Something small, cheap, and not too noisy.'

He laid down the *Preble City Inkling* he'd been reading and strolled around to my side of the counter. 'Who's it for?'

'Me, naturally. You think I'd send it as a birthday present?' I narrowed my eyes at him the way he was narrowing his at me. 'Aren't you Horace Shallenbarger's boy?'

He straightened reflexively, as if being recognized made it necessary to look better. 'Yes. Warren. You taught my twin brother Weldon and I English.'

I winced at another example of my failure. 'Are you going to sell me a gun or not?'

'What do you want a gun for?'

When I go into Tisket Tasket, they don't ask me why I'm buying a dozen eggs and a roll of paper towels,' I growled.

'You don't need a license to possess groceries.'

'Where do I get this license?'

He shambled around to the far side of the counter again brought up a soft-backed book. 'I write you one. If you pass the written test.' He grinned, which made his whiskers splay out like a threatened porcupine. 'Weren't expecting a pop quiz, huh?'

'I'm glad to know a person has to be

lucid enough to answer some questions before you bag his purchase. What information must I master?'

'Name. Address. Phone number. Those are the main things. And I need to see your driver's license. You got one?'

'Certainly,' I said, feeling the old familiar sting of worry it had expired while I wasn't looking. 'Do you want it now?'

'First let's see if there's something here that suits you.' He strolled the length of one wall, me keeping pace on the other side of the glass case, both of us peering in at the massed weapons as if neither of us had seen them before.

Stopping and unlocking the back of a display, he reached in to lift out a platinum-colored gun with a black rubber handle. 'I guess you couldn't hurt yourself much with this little beauty.'

'It's not me I'll be shooting at,' I said, leaning over it with both hands behind my back. A little white price tag was attached to the metal loop protecting the trigger. I could have bought a new refrigerator for the same money.

'It's not loaded, you want to handle it.'

He nudged the pistol at me on the glass.

'Where could I get shooting lessons?' I asked, not touching it.

'I could do it. Twenty bucks an hour is all.'

'I'll take this gun and five dollars' worth of how to shoot it.'

'Do you know how to clean a gun, Miss Quizenberry?' He asked it in the rhetorical way I would have asked him if he knew the past perfect tense of any intransitive verb.

'I assume it's not as simple as putting it on the top rack of the dishwasher,' I said.

'I'll sell you the kit you need. It's got a booklet tells you all about it.'

'Fine.' I hoped the mayor did come after me, to justify all this expense.

We filled out the yellow questionnaire. One of the questions was 'have you ever been arrested,' and I resisted the temptation to answer, 'not yet.'

'I know why you want the gun,' Warren said, tapping the newspaper he'd been reading. 'I've had a bunch of Nervous Nellies in here, thanks to that girl getting herself killed.'

I don't subscribe to *The Preble City Inkling* because the shoddy proofreading outweighed my need to know, and because I could always borrow Velma's copy for free. At the moment, I was rather put out with them for not calling to interview me about finding the body. Of course, I didn't want to comment on it, but they could at least have made the effort.

'When do you want your fifteen-minute cram course?' Warren asked as he watched me write a check.

'As soon as possible. Whenever you can schedule it.'

'Soon, huh? How about after work this afternoon? I close Saturdays at two. I've got a target range in the basement.'

'Lovely.' If fifteen minutes wasn't enough, I could entertain Paul on Sunday with a demonstration of my shooting inability. He would give me lessons for free, if I could tolerate the accompanying censure.

★   ★   ★

I went home and opened my YOW text.

'In writing fiction, don't use the first

95

plot solution that comes into your head. Because it leaps to mind first, it is probably a cliché. Instead, try to think of a more unusual, less traveled path for your story to take.'

In other words, since Jerry Joe was the obvious suspect, it must be someone else who put the lilies in Fuzzy's and Lisa's hands.

I doodled either a long-stemmed lily or a misshapen ax on the waiting sheet of notebook paper. First solution's too easy, eh? Although Jerry Joe was the murderer, I could play a what-if game.

If not Jerry Joe, who? The person had to meet my two-lily criterion: someone with access to Fuzzy the weekend he passed away, and someone who knew Lisa well enough to wish her ill. Another man in Lisa's life. Who also happened to look like a Van Dyke. Jay Jay.

John Junior.

I dropped my poised pen and leaned back in the kitchen chair. Had I been persecuting the wrong Hoffsteder?

No, surely not. John Junior, according to Velma, was farming in Darke County.

Which didn't mean he couldn't visit Preble City and/or Cincinnati any time he so desired.

He was probably married, with a crop of children, a stalwart column of church and community.

I owed it to Jerry Joe to find out.

* * *

The Hoffsteder boys had grown up in a modest ranch-style house in suburban Preble City. Now the elder Hoffsteders lived on twenty acres of prime farm land — which they didn't farm — a couple miles from town. Fortunately, the wrought-iron gate stood open and I scooted the Buick right through and parked on the circle driveway in what would have been the handicapped spot, had this been a public building.

When I rang the doorbell, it bonged the first six notes of the theme from *Rocky*. A brass plate above the button announced *Dr. and Mrs. John Hoffsteder, Sr.* The porch was a stone slab barely large enough to hold a welcome mat, but that was the only thing skimpy about the house. The

Hoffsteder homeplace was one of those stucco and wood-strip Tudors that looks as if it would be hell to paint, with dozens of tall multi-paned windows that look as if they would be hell to wash.

I rang the bell again and easily suppressed the urge to caper about with my arms in the air. Stepping down onto the grass, I bent to diagnose an edging of sweet peas with foot rot. Behind me, the door opened.

'You need some terrazole here,' I said, pointing at the flowers before turning to see whom I was addressing.

It was Jerry Joe's mother, Cynthia. I could tell by the vacant way she gazed at me, one hand to her mouth, the other on her bosom, and the toes of her high-heeled shoes pointing at each other. They say men instinctively search for mates that remind them of their mothers. May Ruth Brock would be a chip off the old mother-in-law.

'Are you selling something?' Cynthia fretted.

'Oh, no. I'm Tirzah Quizenberry. You remember — your children's high school English teacher.'

'Yes?' She looked doubtful. If she had

reservations about what I'd said so far, what would she think when I got to the white lies?

'I'm sorry to bother you, but I need John Junior's address.'

'John Junior?'

'Your oldest,' I reminded gently. 'You see, I was cleaning house, and I came across some things that belong to him — a term paper, a sonnet he wrote after our unit on Shakespeare, a note I confiscated on its way to Annie Beatty. None valuable, but of interest and sentimental value. I hated to simply throw it all away.'

'Oh. Why don't you just give them to me?'

'What a good idea. I didn't bring any of it along, is the trouble. And speaking of trouble, I don't want to make extra for you. I really will drop it all in the mail, if you tell me how to label the envelope.'

She rearranged her feet so that they aimed into the house. 'Come in, I guess.' She widened the door a few inches, flattering me that she thought I'd fit through that narrow an opening.

We jockeyed a bit, and I made it past

her into the cool, dim vestibule. Cynthia led off to the right, into a cool, dim living room. The white carpet was like freshly fallen snow inviting me to walk on it. The nap looked deep enough to lie on one's back and make angels.

'Sit down in that chair,' Cynthia said. The gold and white brocaded wingback was as unyielding as plastic.

She began to sort through a little oak rolltop desk. I hoped that the reason she didn't know John's address was because he telephoned her every week so she wouldn't have to write.

'Does John Junior get back home very often?' I asked.

'Mmm.'

'When was the last time?'

'Uhh.' She stopped pawing to read something on a scrap of blue paper, threw it into the square brass wastebasket, and kept on searching.

'Was he here last Monday, by any chance?'

'Yes.'

'He was!'

She glanced up at my enthusiasm. 'It was my birthday, so he stopped by with a

100

present. A compact disc of Janis Joplin's greatest hits.'

The few times I'd listened to Janis Joplin, I'd felt in need of a bath afterwards. 'How nice. Was Jerry Joe at the party too?' Would this be His Horror's alibi? If I had ever needed an impartial witness, my mother would have been at the very bottom of the list.

'There wasn't any party,' Cynthia said. 'But Jerry Joe did sing 'Happy Birthday' on the telephone. And he sent balloons of course.'

'Of course.'

Cynthia had found something else of interest, a sale flyer for Kmart, it looked like. Dreamily, she scanned the front. Turned the page.

I spoke too loudly, making her start. 'Is John Junior married? Has he children?'

Nodding, she dropped the flyer and finally brought out an address book. It was either that or a pot holder — a five by eight piece of padded blue gingham. It did, in fact, open up to reveal indexed pages. She ran her finger down one.

'Do you have something to write this

on, Miss Quizenberry?' she asked, suddenly briskly in control.

'Just a moment. In here,' I said, taking over the part of rummager, locating notebook in purse. 'Ready.'

'Route One, Greenville, Ohio,' Cynthia said and snapped the book shut.

I stared at her, amazed at the span of her forgetfulness. 'Zip?'

'I don't know. I always call the post office.'

'Perhaps his phone number would be helpful. So I can let him know the package is coming.'

She sighed annoyance, opened the book again, found the page, read it off. I snapped shut my own book and decided to be direct. Poor Cynthia wasn't going to notice that I was shamelessly prying.

'Mrs. Hoffsteder, do you recall the time, years ago, that Jerry Joe brought the class hamster home for a weekend? And the little fellow died?'

Cynthia screwed up her mouth, obediently thinking back. 'Vaguely.'

'Do you vaguely recall what the animal died of?'

'I'm not sure I ever knew. Was it the flu? That was always going around.' She turned away to roll shut the desk. 'I just remember letting Jerry Joe have the box from my new black three-inch heels. I'd got them at The Style Shop. On sale.'

'Please don't take offense now, but . . . ' I stood up to show Cynthia that I was leaving, because people who are about to get something they want tend to speak more freely. 'Do you think John Junior might have had something to do with Fuzzy's demise?'

'Oh, I'll bet he did.' Sure enough, Cynthia's mouth curled into a smile as she showed me to the front door. 'Little John always had a cough or diarrhea or whatever was going around.'

'No, I mean, could he have maybe, accidentally, sort of, wrung the animal's neck? Played too rough, you understand; perhaps Jerry Joe is the one who — '

'Miss Quizen — mmm,' Cynthia swung the door wide, letting in sunlight and the song of a cardinal. 'My boys might have been boys, but they didn't mean anything by it.'

I walked to my car thinking that Cynthia might mean well but she didn't mean much.

Which Hoffsteder brother had been friendly with Lisa Norvell had yet to be established. From the emerging impression I was getting of Lisa, it was likely to be both.

I needed to talk to some more neighbors. Jerry Joe's being handier than John Junior's, that's where I went next.

★　★　★

Jerry Joe's house, bounded by Main Street on the front, Seven Mile Creek on the east, and the Municipal Golf Course on the back, has only one close neighbor — Sylvia Butterbaugh, president of the Garden Club. She doesn't gossip, but a gift cutting from my prize goldfish plant should loosen her tongue.

Just across the bridge, the street was clogged with cars. One of Sylvia's garage sales seemed to be the attraction. I crept past, turned around in the country club's driveway, crossed the bridge again, and parked on the other side.

As I strolled toward Sylvia's, I paused to enjoy the cooler air and slightly fishy scent above the creek. A solitary white duck bobbed for minnows, unperturbed by a beer can floating past to the sea. On the horizon, a trio of people stood around in attitudes of casual assurance; a fourth twisted violently as if under torture, his club and ball invisible.

I inspected Jerry Joe's house as I passed. A turn-of-the-century one-and-a-half story, it's about the same vintage as mine. But whereas my white clapboard has a token front porch and no gingerbread, Jerry Joe's vernacular wood-frame is a dolls' house of peach and gray and maroon fish-scale shingles, gabled and chimneyed and verandaed on three sides. My house is plain white bread; Jerry Joe's is jelly donut.

He wasn't anywhere in sight, and the doors and windows were closed.

In contrast, Sylvia's driveway looked as if the garage had exploded onto it; assorted strangers picked through the debris. I strolled up the concrete, pretending interest in the wares.

Sylvia didn't operate your usual garage sale: 1. Items might be bargains, but they weren't cheap. 2. She wouldn't haggle; her policy remained take it or leave it, even if the sun was beginning to set and she wanted to go inside to watch *Senior Showcase*. She'd rather keep anything that didn't sell and try again next time.

And so I recognized an umbrella stand made of elephant hair, and a raw umber phallic vase with no redeeming social value, both of which were more likely to sprout legs and crawl off than ever be sold at any price. A small crowd milled around Sylvia's ever popular carton of found golf balls. As always, the sign said, 'Ten cents each. Any you can prove are yours: five cents.'

The proprietress sat in an aluminum and webbing lawn chair within the line of shade inside the garage, coffee mug in one hand and cigarette in the other. She wore a white shirt, a blue bandanna neck scarf, and slacks the same shade of lavender as her frowzy hair.

'Tirzzy,' she acknowledged me without smiling. She knew from past experience I wasn't going to cross her palm with silver or better.

'Sylvia,' I said. 'You picked a nice day.'

Deeper in the garage, Sylvia's daughter-in-law bent from the waist, trying to drag a Seagram's box of paperbacks out into the light for an interested customer. Above the squeal of cardboard on gritty concrete, she declared, 'Romances, mysteries, science fiction, and a soupcon of Westerns.'

'I finally remembered to bring you the goldfish cutting you wanted,' I said to Sylvia, scooping it out of the mouth of my purse.

'My, my, my. That's something.' Her mouth twisted into a grin as she stuck her cigarette into it and reverently lifted the delicate plastic-bagged shoot out of my hand. 'Let's put this in water, post quick,' she said, squinting, the cigarette snapping up and down to the words.

We went through the little door at the back of the garage, into the quiet, neat, cinnamon-scented kitchen. I walked to the bay window breakfast nook that overlooked the bird feeder. If I craned sideways, I could see Jerry Joe's back yard, separated from Sylvia's by a grape arbor and a row of raspberries. He wasn't over there, but his lawn mower sat out in the middle of dual-level grass, like an interrupted haircut.

Sylvia ran water into a Mason jar and eased the goldfish shot into it. 'Thank you, Tirzzy. I'd about given up on your remembering this.'

I felt a pang of shame for failing to please her sooner, before I had an ulterior motive for doing it. Knowing she'd hustle me out as readily as she'd let me in, I came straight to the point.

'Is Jerry Joe all right? Looks like he left off mowing in a rush.'

'He drove off with May Ruth a while ago, probably for lunch.' Sylvia foraged through the leaves, obviously inspecting for parasites and fungi.

'What does Jerry Joe do for a living? Being mayor isn't a full-time job.'

'He owns part interest in a beer distributorship.'

'Huh. Maybe that's how he got acquainted with Lisa Norvell,' I thought out loud. 'Maybe he distributed beer to place she worked. Sylvia, did you ever see Lisa Norvell over there at his house?'

Sylvia looked up, her eyes the preoccupied blank of someone who hasn't been listening. 'Who?'

'I was wondering if you'd ever seen that murdered girl. At Jerry Joe's, maybe.'

She shook her head, baffled by the subject. 'When?'

'I don't know.' I threw both hands up. 'Ever.'

'Why?'

'I'm curious is all.'

She set her mouth in a disapproving line and deposited the glass jar on the windowsill over the sink. It was not her nature to rock boats, step on toes, or ruffle feathers. I could see she was going to be her usually honorable self, which always seems to bring out the baser traits of anyone around her. Mine, anyway.

'Sylvia, for May Ruth's sake, have you noticed Jerry Joe visiting with another female in the last several months?'

'Tirzzy Quizenberry. You aren't usually the one to tittle-tattle,' she scolded.

'Does that mean 'yes'?'

Sighing out smoke, she flapped both hands at me, herding me toward the door. 'It means I've got better things to do.'

I grabbed hold of the doorjamb as she tried to nudge me out. 'No, listen. This is important. Life or death, mostly death. Did you ever hear Jerry Joe fighting with anyone?'

'Never.' The flat of her hand relentlessly urged me onward. 'Well, maybe once.' She passed me on the left, moving purposefully toward a prospective buyer of ugly vases. 'There was one time he sounded really put out that this woman — a golfer, apparently — had more balls than he did.'

★　★　★

I was beginning to feel mild stirrings of panic over not yet having written anything worthwhile for Marvin Golden and Your Own Write. It took me back to my college days, when I'd put off studying for a test too long and then couldn't concentrate because my mind was counting the seconds ticking relentlessly out from under me.

Sitting at the kitchen table, I let the text fall open where it would.

'It is fun to write light, humorous poetry. Usually these works will be rhymed and metered (see previous page) to give the rollicking, lyrical beat that adds to a happy poem's appeal. Write such a poem about an animal, using all the senses including nonsense.'

There once was a hamster named
  Fuzzy —
[So far, so good, Tirzzy — you can do it.]
There once was a hamster named Fuzzy,
Whose fate to this day remains muzzy.
He died on a visit,
But which brother is it,
Who turned Fuzzy from izzy to wuzzy?

Imagining Mr. Golden's puckered face as he tried to interpret this, I tucked it into the pocket of my blue buckram notebook and pulled the textbook under my nose again.

'Serious poetry is most often, these

days, free verse (see previous page). Shut your eyes for a moment. What is the one most dominant feeling that floods into your mind? Write a short, honest poem about it.'

Obediently I closed my eyes and waited for inspiration. The refrigerator cycled off. The abrupt quiet was nudged by a rumble of thunder, miles to the north. I smelled honeysuckle. What did I feel? Sleepy.

There was an old woman named Teepee —

Opening my eyes before I should doze off, I picked up the YOW pen and felt the familiar pinch at the base of that thumb. When I spread my hands as if to play piano, the fingers reminded me of node-heavy carnation stems. I repositioned the pen and began to write.

> *— Like a werewolf reacting to the*
> *globose moon,*
> *I flex my hands and see*
> *The changes, day to month:*
> *The curling in,*
> *The twisting down,*
> *The claw forming.*

A knee cracks.
A hipbone seizes in dry socket.
An ankle hauls afoot in shambling stride.
Unlike the slavering, gleam-eyed wolf,
It isn't blood I crave.

Well double drat. I couldn't send whippersnapper Golden this drivel.

Removing my glasses to swipe impatiently at my blurry eyes, I shoved chair away from table and tried to decide what to serve Paul McMorris for dinner tomorrow. But before I'd got up to speed and past the cauliflower-pea salad, the clock striking in the living room announced it was time to go have a sharpshooting lesson.

6

'Watch your step, Ms. Quizenberry,' Warren said, going sideways down the stone stairs so that he could monitor my progress. The guardrail felt as if it could use a good dose of Pledge.

As we descended, the bare ceiling bulb at the top of the flight stretched our shadows ahead of us into long black monsters. Warren carried my new gun, and at the foot of the steps he used the bottom edge of the handle to activate a different light switch. It irritated me that he was so cavalier with my property.

This new illumination was still no better than a 60-watt bulb in a black expanse of basement islanded by building supports and stacked cartons. Warren led off across the dirt floor, telling me again to mind how I walked.

I did mind. I hated it, the treacherous footing and the poor visibility. Twenty years ago, I wouldn't have dared to come down here alone with Warren at all.

We traversed the sea of cellar to yet another light switch beside a slab of wooden door. Again, Warren used the gun where a bare finger would have done, and when he creaked the door open, we were dazzled by a big bright bowling-alley of a room with a wooden fence at the near end. At the far end were posters with bull's eyes or silhouettes of men or deer. The ones depicting men had been shot up the most. Warren laid my gun on a ledge in front of the fence and opened the box of ammunition for me. He loaded eight of what he called three-eighty supers into what he called the mag, and snapped that into the handle of what he called a 'Retta. Then he let all that work go to waste by reversing the procedure, shaking the bullets into their cardboard box, and handing the gun to me.

'Now you do it.'

By the time I'd pincered those shiny little torpedoes into their berths, my arthritis had me mad enough to shoot anything that moved.

Warren said, 'The first time you pull,

you're cocking it. Then it will fire a bullet every time you pull the trigger. To put the safety on, you do this.' He did it twice. 'Understand?'

I nodded, feeling like the time my seventh-grade science teacher made us hold a live snake.

My current instructor showed me how to point the 'Retta two-handed, the way people do it on TV, and sight through a notch the size of the hole in a darning needle. Warren told me to aim at the middle target, which was so far away I'd have had trouble making out the bull, let alone the eye. Then he snapped a pair of black leather earmuffs on me and yelled, 'Go ahead.'

I squeezed the trigger, trying to keep my arms from weaving. The thing pulled so hard, I wanted to tuck it tween my knees for extra leverage. When the explosion finally came, I'd given up trying to sight. It was a surprise to see an upper corner of the paper target fly into the air.

'That's good,' Warren said. 'Now bring it down about a foot.'

Knowing this time how loud it was

going to be, I wasn't quite as squeamish about squeezing off a second shot. It nicked the bottom edge of the paper. Taking a deep breath of gunpowder scent, I throttled off one more.

'Where did that one hit?' I shouted, as if I were so interested I had to lower the pistol and my aching arms for a few moments waiting for an answer.

'Bottom left outer ring. Looking good, Miss Quizenberry.'

'How many minutes do I have left?'

'Don't worry about it.' Warren waved a magnanimous hand. 'I'll give you some extra if I have to. Go ahead and empty the magazine.'

Refreshed by this little rest, I hefted the pistol and shot three more times. They all hit the paper. Somewhere.

Resting again, I said, 'Now that I've mastered this, do you want to teach me to fast draw?'

He opened his mouth to talk me out of it before he realized I was kidding.

Two more bullets and I could go home. I took my stance, squinted through the little green notch, and pulled twice in succession.

'Oh wow,' Warren said. 'You're this close.'

I peeled the earmuffs off my head. 'To being in the bull's eye?'

'To being on the paper.'

'That's good enough,' I said. 'I probably won't ever fire it again anyway.'

He put the gun into its brass-hinged vinyl case for me. 'Hope you don't. I hope buying it was just a big waste of your money.' His rosy lips grinned inside their nest of hair. 'That's what I told that Ms. Norvell.'

I'd been flexing my fingers to get the cramp out, and I froze like a surgeon waiting for his rubber glove. As casually as I could manage, I said, 'You sold a gun to Lisa Norvell?'

Warren's eyes gleamed with suppressed confidences. 'One week ago this coming Monday.'

'Did you tell the police?'

He shrugged, still looking mischievous. 'Why? They're looking for the murder weapon, and they know it's a 9mm caliber. What good would it do to speculate that it was the one she bought from me?'

'Well, I don't know. But every scrap of

information is bound to add to the total picture.'

He shrugged again, and we began walking into the darker part of the basement. When he shut off the firing range lights, the blackness was like a tide slapping over us.

Ignoring the urge to run for higher ground, I said, 'Was she alone when she bought the gun?'

'Yes. Attractive young lady driving a red Jeep. Nobody in it waiting for her.'

'Why did she want a gun?'

'The Tisket Tasket doesn't pry into their customers' private lives,' he mock-reminded me.

'Come on, Warren. She must have said something.'

'She said . . . ' He touched my elbow, indicating the bottom step. I glanced up at the top where the afternoon sun painted the ceiling gold.

Warren climbed companionably beside me, finishing his sentence. ' . . . it was for protection against rats.'

I felt a surge of kinship for poor Lisa. 'Have you got another other gun like the one you sold her?'

'Happen I do. Nice little 3913 S and W double action. Bought the both of them used, at a gun show in Columbus.'

'I want to see it.'

We hauled ourselves to the lip of the staircase and Warren pointed me left. Halfway to the front door, he stopped at a display case and pointed again. The gray and silver pistol was about the size of my new weapon, and just as evil-looking.

'I want to exchange this gun you just sold me for one like that,' I said.

Warren didn't groan, but he ran his hand across the top of his head and rocked from foot to foot. 'What do you want to do that for? All the paperwork would have to be done over, and I got an appointment in a few minutes.'

He said that last with the same earnest inflection he used to use when he needed to use the restroom as soon as I announced a pop quiz.

I hardened my heart now as I had then. 'This gun here the one I'll take, Warren. And you can just tell me how to operate it. No need to traipse back to the basement.'

I wasn't sure why it was important that I have a gun like the one that had surely killed Lisa. It seemed right and fitting, somehow.

And besides, it was five dollars cheaper than the 'Retta.

★　★　★

The telephone rang, sudden and ugly as a buzzsaw by my car. I floundered up out of the sheets and lunged to take it off the cradle.

'Hello!'

'Hello, Mrs. Quizenberry. This is Jerry Joe Hoffsteder. I thought I'd save you the trouble of calling me tonight by calling you first.'

The digital clock said 1:50.

'How nice of you,' I said as jovially as I could manage, determined not to let him hear he'd rattled me. 'As it happens, I wasn't intending to phone you tonight. I had the impression you didn't want to be disturbed.'

'Nonsense. A good politician expects to be a disturbed human being.'

'Well put,' I said, hitching higher in the bed and battling my twisted nightgown into place.

'So you didn't have anything to discuss with me tonight? If not, I'm going to bed now, and I'm going to pull out the telephone plug to ward off wrong numbers and thoughtless pranksters.'

'Good idea. I'm tempted to do the same.'

Instead of disconnecting the telephone, I switched on the bedside lamp and double-checked that my new S and W double action 3913 hadn't evaporated from the nightstand drawer.

★　★　★

Sunday. The Church of Christ bell rang and the Methodist loudspeaker played organ hymns, like two people arguing without listening to each other.

I was brought up Presbyterian, embraced Unitarianism during my college years, and deteriorated into Agnosticism after the war. Now if someone is rude enough to ask, I say that I'm a devout Abecedarian or a born-again Expostulate or something else nonsensical but true.

If we really wanted to humble ourselves before a Lord, we'd go to church naked.

I donned my pink flowered double-knit dress and white canvas apron and spent the morning making Three Layer Salad, One-Rise Rolls, and Chocolate Cake with Cream Cheese Icing. My cooking is like my love life: just because I don't, doesn't mean I can't.

While things were marinating, rising and cooling, I flapped open the Sunday *Cincinnati Enquirer* and browsed, alert for any reference to Preble City's murder. I take the *Enquirer* Sundays only, so I'd missed whatever might have been in it Tuesday. I could have bought a single copy from a news rack. But why waste fifty cents to read secondhand what I'd experienced firsthand? Anyway, there was no mention of Lisa a scant week after her terrible experience.

Through the open windows, the tentative grumbling of Velma's old Ford indicated her return home from church. I went out the kitchen screen door onto my little square porch and waited till she'd shut off the engine, escaped the seat belt, and hauled herself clear of the car.

'Hey, Velma! Have a cup of coffee?'

'Not with me,' she joked, crossing the two driveways and marching up my steps.

She sank onto a kitchen chair with a whoosh of breath and fanned at her neck with her black clutch purse.

'You want it iced?' I offered.

'That would be lovely. I like your perfume.'

'It's just the same old lily of the valley.'

'No. Chocolate and yeast. Who's coming for lunch?'

I waved a carelessly dismissive hand. 'Paul McMorris.'

She nodded and dropped one eyelid. 'A private detective has to stay on the good side of a policeman. Through this stomach.'

Making a face at the unpleasant image she'd conjured, I poured warm coffee slowly over the ice cubes in two glasses. The ice crackled and popped.

'So what's on your schedule this week?' I asked, handing Velma one glass and the sugar bowl.

'Not much except it's my turn to have Garden Club. Oh, and Yappy's due for a rabies booster. You think it's too hot for Mexican?'

'Mexican what?'

'Mexican food. At the meeting. Jimmy-changas, or whatever.'

But I hadn't followed this branch of the dialogue. I was still back at Yappy's inoculation. 'Velma — who's your veterinarian?'

'Wayne Trum. It used to be Sherry Berryman until her husband tested allergic to animal dander and she had to find another line of — '

'Did you ever take Yappy to Dr. Hoffsteder?'

Velma gave a theatrical shiver. 'No. I only tell Yap I'm going to if he's being bad.'

'Oh, come on. Dr. H. has a perfectly respectable professional reputation.'

'So does Wayne Trum. You need anyone to lick the icing beaters?'

'Listen, Velma. Why don't you take Yappy to Hoffsteder just this one time? And I'll go with you.'

'Why? You think we can threaten the

old man into saying his son killed that girl? Turn Yappy loose on him if he doesn't cooperate?'

'I don't know what I hope to learn. But making the appointment with him instead of Trum couldn't hurt anything, could it?'

'If their rates are the same.'

'I'll pay the difference if it's more.' I cut a big divot out the cake and put it on a paper plate for her to take home.

* * *

'Delicious cake,' Paul McMorris said, dabbing at his mouth with my grandmother's hand-embroidered linen napkin. 'Delicious everything.' He leaned back, rubbing one hand appreciatively across his midsection.

'It's going to cost you,' I said, elbows on the table, coffee cup poised at my chin. 'I'd like to take a ride.'

'Oh? Where would you like to go?'

'Up to Darke County to see where John Hoffsteder, Junior lives.'

Paul frowned. 'What's this got to do with your Jerry Joe obsession?'

'It's not an obsession. In fact, I'm willing to concede that Jerry Joe may not be the murderer at all.'

'Yeah?' He eyed me with hope adulterated by disbelief.

'You were right. I accused him prematurely.'

'Yeah?' The hope expanded an atom.

'John Junior had as much opportunity, motive, and relevant initials as his brother.'

Paul groaned. 'Isn't there some other hobby you could take up, Tirzzy? Something as challenging as sleuthing but less dangerous? Stock car racing, perhaps?'

I stood and collected crumb-speckled plates. 'If I can tell you something you don't know about the case, will you help me interview John Junior?'

'Tirzzy,' he said sternly, 'withholding evidence is not a bargaining tool. It's a punishable offense.'

'Pooh,' I said, clapping the lid onto the layer cake as if it were trying to escape. 'There's such a thing as informers. They get paid for what they can tell the police. All I want is a Sunday drive in the country.'

Standing and bringing his empty cup

and saucer to the sink, Paul leaned his face at mine. 'What's your belch?'

'Beg pardon?' I blinked, but I didn't flinch as he swayed closer yet. He smelled of cigar smoke and coffee.

'You want to be an informer? The slang is.'

'Oh, really?' Delighted, I reached for the buckram notebook I had relegated to the top of the refrigerator during meal preparations. 'Let me just jot that down.'

I could see he was disappointed that his theatrics hadn't frightened or disgusted me. Finishing my notation with a flourish, I said, 'Lisa Norvell bought a Smith and Wesson pistol, model 3913, the morning of the day she was shot.'

It was a wonderful moment. Like the time my sister and I surprised Dad with all As on both our report cards. Paul's eyes got that same dazed glassiness, while his lips gradually curled upwards.

'How'd you know that?'

'I asked the man at High Noon Firearms.'

'Huh. Nice going, Tirzzy. I should have thought of doing that myself.'

'Yes, you should have,' I supported him completely.

★ ★ ★

'Lisa Norvell's Jeep is missing. Tracks in the Linebarger yard indicate it was parked there at some time. Logic says it was the evening she was killed, and whoever killed her took it.'

We were in Paul's black Taurus on our way to John Junior's, and Paul was sharing what the investigation had turned up so far. I could picture the Lisa Norvell file folder on his desk, its partial page of typed notes having grown to — oh, at least two pages.

The sky had turned dishwater gray, trying to work up a good shower. Corn marched calf-high in most of the fields. Sweet clover, soybeans, or an occasional harem of cows occupied other acreage. We swooped over a county road dip, as tummy-tickling as a kiddy roller coaster.

I had a map across my knees, mostly to keep the air conditioning off my legs. We knew approximately where we were going, Paul having telephoned John Junior for directions before we embarked. Our rather flimsy excuse for the visit was the high school term paper I'd found in my attic. I really did have a term paper in my purse.

'Have you formulated any suspects at all?' I asked, emphasizing the 'you.'

'There was a transient in the neighborhood the Sunday before. Could be he was camping at the Linebarger house and Lisa surprised him. Though what she was doing there, we haven't established.'

'Picking tiger lilies,' I couldn't help jibing.

'We'll find him. He'll be driving her truck, using her credit cards, bragging in taverns that he killed a woman. Want to bet me another homemade dinner?' He turned his face to grin at me.

'I hope you know how to make cabbage rolls, because that's what I want when you have to pay up,' I answered tartly.

Still smiling, Paul straightened around and fished in his shirt pocket for an index card — the one he'd appropriated from my kitchen drawer — and checked our progress on the map he'd drawn on it. A family of quails churned across the road, their legs blurs of forward progress. Paul put his foot on the brake to make a right-hand turn.

'The first lane. About half a mile,' Paul deciphered his notes, then stuffed the card into his pocket again.

One side of the narrow road was striped with corn rows, the other was a smorgasbord of grasses and weeds for eight Jersey cows and a pony. At the top of a gradual rise, house, barn, and outbuildings huddled together under tulip trees full of dead wood. When we slowed at the nameless mailbox to swing into the gravel lane, two black dogs with threadbare plumy tails trotted from the barnyard to challenge us, one a baritone and one a bass.

Three people stood around a cultivator on the weedy gravel apron to the barn. They all turned and stared as we rolled to a stop. Paul put his side window at half-mast and shouted over the dogs. 'Mr. Hoffsteder?'

One figure detached himself from the

trio and walked toward us, wiping his grease-blackened hands on an old — I hoped — tea towel. He snarled at the dogs, something and all a's and r's, and they both lay down as if the power had been cut off.

'Help you?' the man said, methodically working between each finger of the right hand.

'I'm Paul McMorris, and you know Mrs. Quizenberry.'

Both of us were climbing out the car now that the threat of being dog chow had dissipated.

'Lordy. It's been a spell, Mrs. Q,' John Junior said, stretching out a hand to shake Paul's. I offered my hand too, though I worried that it wasn't as pristine as John Junior's must be after all that polishing. 'Lessee — I graduated in 1962, so that makes it . . . ' He swallowed the answer and turned to motion for his wife. Having never taught any math, I didn't feel my usual disappointment in manifest inadequacy.

'Hurry up, here, Bonita. Come meet my old English teacher.'

I doubt he meant it disrespectfully.

John Junior took off his John Deere cap to swipe at his sweat-damp hair. I'm not familiar with Jerry Van Dyke, but if there are similarities, he must be a stocky, big-headed man with a pleasant grin. John Junior had a farmer's yin-yang complexion — ruddy from the eyebrows down, dead white above, giving the impression his face was only three quarters full.

The woman had finally strolled into conversation range. She wore baggy blue jeans and a Garst Seed T-shirt. Looking farm-wife capable of baking pies or driving combines, she smiled the reluctant way people do when they want to be somewhere else.

'Mrs. Quizenberry, Bonita went to school in Warren Township,' John Junior said by way of introduction.

'How do you do,' I said, nodding instead of extending my hand, afraid she would jump back if I made that kind of move. 'John, I have a hard time keeping tabs on all my former students. Have you been married long?'

'Twenty years?' John Junior guessed,

looking at his wife for confirmation.

She snickered. 'Darrell is twenty-four.'

John Junior rubbed ruefully at his cheek. 'Darrell's our son,' he explained unnecessarily, twisting to look at the barn. 'Don't know where he went. Anyway, if he's twenty-four, we must be married, lessee, uhh — '

The gray sky began to spit rain at us. The Hoffsteders did ask us into the house. They did ease back toward the yawning barn door, and Paul and I eased with them.

'So did you really drive all the way from Preble City just to give me some old homework papers?' John Junior marveled.

'Mostly we wanted to take a Sunday drive.' I watched the bare ground break out in polka dots, breathing the wonderful new-rain scent. If Estee Lauder could bottle that, I'd buy it by the quart.

All of us stopped on the sill of the open barn. It was one of the new kind — metal walls and concrete floor — a poor substitute for the real all-wood barns of the good old days. Still, it smelled right. Like hay and manure.

Parked facing us was a dusty tractor the size of a greater dinosaur. Something flashed behind the windshield, and then the door bumped open and a shrill voice shouted, 'Grampa?'

A tiny body slithered down the side of the cab and galloped toward us. The two dogs brushed past me and wagged a welcome as they met the child. She raised both elbows out of the way, standing tiptoe, as they snuffled at her.

'This is Heidi,' John Junior said, walking over to lift her up and sit her against his chest. 'Darrell's daughter.' He nuzzled her neck, making her squeal.

The rain stopped pussy-footing around, and we all crowded into the barn, turning to look at the downpour as if we'd never seen one.

'I wanta get wet,' Heidi announced, wriggling in John Junior's arms till he set her down. She capered outdoors, blond-ringleted head tipped back, tongue out, sun-colored arms spread wide to welcome the soaking.

'How old is she?' Paul asked.

'Almost three,' John Junior said without

any figuring or consulting with his wife. 'She's a pistol.'

The substantive compliment reminded me to get down to business. I began searching my purse for the alleged term paper. 'Paul, didn't you want to ask John Junior about something?'

7

'Mr. Hoffsteder, I'm with the Preble City Police Department,' Paul began. 'I'm working on the Lisa Norvell murder case. You've probably heard about it.'

'Yes,' John Junior said doubtfully.

Bonita, who'd been a decidedly reluctant member of our group, backed farther into the barn, arms folded, face blank of interest or emotion.

Paul said, 'I understand you were out and about in our town on Monday, the evening it happened, so naturally I wondered if you might have seen anything unusual.'

'No, I don't believe so.' John Junior frowned as if to demonstrate that his prompt answer didn't mean he was unsympathetic.

'Whereabouts were you at, say, ten o'clock or later?' Paul smiled to demonstrate he wasn't threatening anybody.

'Bonita and the kids and I were at Mother Hoffsteder's from about seven to ten, ten thirty, and then we drove home. We weren't anywhere near the Linebarger place. Afraid we can't help you.'

'By kids, you mean — '

'Heidi and her dad.' John Junior glanced out at the yard where the little girl still danced in the rain. 'Heidi's mama is dead.'

'Sorry to hear it,' Paul murmured.

'Oh, how sad,' I said. 'Was she ill?' My regret was genuine; it softened the impertinence of the question, I hoped.

'Auto accident,' John Junior answered curtly. His face smoothed out, and he nodded at my hand holding the notebook paper from my attic. 'Is that the antique English assignment?'

'Oh. Yes, of course.'

'You could have just pitched it in the nearest trash can. I expect that's what I'll do with it.' He took the yellowed papers and tipped them toward the doorway's watery light.

''Food Metaphors in *Romeo and Juliet*.' I don't remember this.'

'Isn't it funny how thoroughly we forget things that were of major concern to us as children?'

'I don't even remember reading *Romeo and Juliet*,' John Junior marveled. 'An A-plus? Are you sure this is mine? It isn't my handwriting.' He squinted closer at the top of the page. 'Looks like the name was erased and mine printed in.'

'Really? Well, why would anyone do that? Here, I'll just take it home with me, to read again sometime. The topic sounds interesting.' At least I'd thought so fifty-some years ago when I wrote it for my English teacher.

The beating rain hesitated and eased off. We all watched Heidi trying to turn a cartwheel over a mud puddle. The silence stretched.

'You ready to go, Tirzzy?' Paul said.

I felt opportunity leeching away like the water in the grass. 'I believe so.' Shuffling a few steps, I turned and looked our host in the eye. 'John, did you happen to know Lisa Norvell — the woman who was killed?'

He didn't bat a lid, answering promptly, 'No, ma'am, I don't believe so.'

Across his shoulder, his wife gazed at me, not batting anything either.

Across her shoulder, in the depths of the gloomy barn, a pale face stared at me momentarily and then floated away. Son Darrell, I presumed, and not a ghost. Still, my heart went haywire for a moment.

His scowl was as hate-filled as a tent of bigots.

*　　*　　*

'Did you learn anything, Tirzzy? Was it worth the trip?' Paul squirmed, uncomfortable in his rain-wet seat, a consequence of our forgetting about the rolled-down window.

'Oh, yes, I learned a great deal. I just don't know means quite yet.'

We were traveling southwest toward the sun, which still wore a dirty film of high clouds. The wet pavement hissed at our tires. The fields smelled steamy and green.

I tipped back my head and shut my eyes, suddenly tired. Darrell's evil eye at work? What had I done to incite his malice? I considered asking Paul's opinion, but it was too much trouble, and I slept instead.

★ ★ ★

'Home again, jiggedy jog,' Paul announced, bringing the car to a gentle stop in my driveway.

'Will you come in for a cup of coffee?' I asked, my social instincts immediately alert though my brain still idled awake.

'No, thank you. I'll see you to the door, though.'

'Never mind. I remember where it is.' I exited the Ford briskly, to forestall any old-fashioned chivalry. Through Paul's open window, we exchanged enough thank-yous and smiles and see-you-soons to choke a cat.

I whistled the whole time it took me to clean up the dishes, mostly Cole Porter.

★ ★ ★

'Pretend that you are someone else who is nothing like you,' my YOW textbook commanded. 'Now write entries for an imaginary diary this person is keeping. Be careful that the real you doesn't wrest control away from temporary guest inside your mind.'

My name is Lisa Norvell. I am young and very pretty and too daring for my own good. I think I can take care of myself because I've been doing it since I was a teen, when our parents deserted my brother and me. I enjoy being a girl. Men are such [expletive deleted]; they're definitely the weaker sex. Whiners and liars and egotists. Forever babies stalled at the oral stage, smoking and drinking and mouthing off.

And kissing. And so forth. It's good old so forth that makes them worth the trouble. Shut my ears, I can have a prime time with the opposite sex.

Trouble is, I come on too strong for some of them. I'm not afraid to say what's on my mind. I get ideas on how to improve my life and I go for it. Even if the ideas involve something a little shady. Like blackmail.

I'm smart enough to buy myself a gun before I issue my demands. But overconfidence drops my guard, does me in. This one particular man, Jay Jay, turns and fights. For his political reputation and his pending marriage? Or for his placid life on the family farm?

Anyway, now I'm dead, because one of 'my' men had more on the balls [sic] than I gave him credit for.

I put down my pen, ears feeling hot. That was as long as I could undertake Lisa's persona. And although I thought I'd been most empathic, here was yet another assignment I couldn't possibly share with Mr. Golden.

★   ★   ★

The telephone brayed, jerking me out of sleep.

I flailed around for the receiver and knocked it off the cradle. Reeling it back by the springy cord, I finally told it, 'Hello.'

'Hello, Mrs. Quizenberry,' Jerry Joe greeted me as cheerfully as an aluminum siding salesman. 'How are you doing?'

'Doing what?' I mumbled, squinting at the clock. Two-thirty-six.

'Say, I know it's late, but I'd like to drop by the house and talk to you.'

'What about?' My voice was finally up to speed, and my wits were close behind.

143

'What about? Oh, potholes, historical preservation, your life's savings. Murder. Whatever topic seems the most promising.'

So the harasser was to be the harassed.

'Mrs. Quizenberry? You still there?'

'Jerry Joe, I'd love to chat with you,' I said, and then nerve failed me. 'But it wouldn't be proper for you to drop in this late. Why don't you come to lunch tomorrow?'

I could use up the Sunday leftovers on him.

There was a breathing silence on the line. Then he said in the same hearty tone, 'Sorry, I can't make it tomorrow. I'll give you another call soon.'

'Not if I call you first,' was my lame retort.

★ ★ ★

Monday morning. I was watering my flame violet, giving it a pep talk about blooming again, when Velma came to the back door. She rapped and walked in, not in that order.

144

'I made an appointment for Yappy with Dr. Hoffsteder. You owe me another lobster dinner.'

'Okay. How soon could he work you in?'

'Two o'clock.'

'Today? It's not an emergency rabies booster is it?'

'No, and that's exactly why I don't like the idea of taking Yap to him. If his appointment book isn't filled past one thirty today, what does that say about the man's practice?'

'Maybe he had a cancellation.'

'Well, I've half a mind to give him another one.'

'I'll drive,' I said.

★ ★ ★

Wayne Trum's animal hospital is in the back rooms of his old farm house out on Oxtail Road. John Hoffsteder's practice is in a new pseudo-Colonial building next door to the First National Bank on Main Street. That pretty much sums up the difference between their bedside manners.

Yappy trotted cheerfully into the back seat of my car, and he even held reasonably still for Velma to snap on his leash while I do-si-doed the Buick into a parallel parking place in front of Hoffsteder's office. But as soon as we stepped into the waiting room, Yap's sense of smell woke him to the reality of the situation; he sat down and grabbed the carpet with all four paws.

The woman behind the receptionist counter island glanced up and nodded. 'Mrs. Newby?'

Grunting with the effort of picking up a dog whose body had developed St. Vitus's dance, Velma nodded.

'Please have a seat. Doctor will be with you in a moment.' I'd heard that line before. I chose the least uncomfortable-looking chair and settled down, ankles and arms crossed, to survey the room.

It was navy-blue and orange. Oak and glass. Paintings of mountains and oceans. Green plants. And not another patient in sight.

Velma had managed to wrestle Yappy within reach of a chair. She looped the leash around one of its legs and sat on the seat. Giving up, the dog huddled against her shins, shivering intermittently like a badly tuned engine.

'I know, I know,' Velma soothed. 'It's exactly how I feel at the gynecologist's.'

The receptionist came out to us through a cleverly concealed swing door, bearing a clipboard and a ballpoint pen. She clicked the latter while she talked to us — in-out, in-out — until I yearned to grab her hand and confiscate the thing.

'You haven't brought your toy terrier in before? If not, I need you to fill out this questionnaire.'

'This was Tirzzy's idea,' Velma said. 'Can't she fill it out?'

The woman squinted at me. 'Aren't you Tirzah Quizenberry?'

'Yes, and you must be Rosie Hoffst-eder. Or is it some other last name now?'

Jerry Joe and John Junior's sister shook her head. 'Hoffsteder,' she agreed, not looking too thrilled about it.

If I hadn't been expecting to see her here, I wouldn't have recognized her. The Rosie I'd had in school was pudgy and plain. This Rosie was thin and fancy. Fancy from the neck up, at least. Pancaked and mascaraed and blushed and perfumed. Her dark, glossy hair was sliced off about the same length all around, exposing shave stubble on the back of her neck and concealing her eyebrows in front. When she moved her eyes, wisps of bangs caught in her lashes. She looked about forty going on twenty-nine.

Handing the clipboard and, mercifully, the pen to Velma, she walked back to her station, blue nylon pant uniform swishing.

Velma began to fill in blanks. ''Age'. Mine or Yappy's?'

'Yappy's would be more relevant,' I said.

'Nine,' she said as she wrote it. ''Reason for visit?' My crazy neighbor.' I don't think that's what she actually penned in.

In the distance, a door slammed and a dog barked. He must have said something interesting — Yappy sat up straighter and opened his ears.

A heavyset woman came from the back carrying a white kitten. While their bill was being settled, Dr. Hoffsteder loomed into view and motioned at us.

'You want to come in, Tirzzy?' Velma asked, unwinding the leash and scooping up Yappy, who began to hyperventilate.

'It would look a little strange, two of us to one little dog.' I stood up.

'Come on then,' she said.

Hoffsteder's interest licked across each of us as we filed past him into the examining cubicle. Velma sat Yappy on a chrome table and snugged up the leash to keep him there, an unwilling centerpiece. I sat down in a straight chair in the corner, under a poster warning of feline urinary tract disorders.

Closing the door, Hoffsteder circled to the far side of the table and leaned over Yappy. The man's shaggy eyebrows and beady eyes hadn't improved with age. He'd begun to stoop under the weight of years, but his shoulders were still broad and meaty. He held out a hand for Yappy to sniff, and both it and the dog trembled.

'Just a routine rabies booster?' the doctor rumbled, glancing again at superfluous me.

'Yes,' Velma said. 'That will be all today, thank you.'

He turned around to take something from a chrome cabinet. Was I going to waste my time sitting here like a tick on a turnip?

'Dr. Hoffsteder, I'm Tirzzy Quizenberry. Remember me?'

'Umff,' he said, not looking around. He and Cynthia must have wonderfully stimulating discussions at the dinner table.

'I'm going to write a series of articles about local businesses for the Garden Club newsletter. Would you mind if I did one on you?'

'Don't have time,' he said, and Velma rolled her eyes as we both thought about how fast she'd booked this appointment.

'I wouldn't need to bother you,' I said. 'I could just ask Rosie a question or two.'

He swiveled toward us again, flourishing a gleaming hypodermic needle. Not counting him, three of us took deep breaths.

Although I was the one with the least at stake, I'm the one who succumbed to cowardice. 'I'll just slip out and look for Rosie.'

Retreating into the little hall, I shut the

door against my heels and smiled in the direction of the waiting room. Rosie wasn't at her post. Blinking twice to be sure I hadn't overlooked her, I twisted to sight the other direction of the hallway. At the far end, past what must be other examining room doors, was a larger door labeled *Private*.

'Rosie,' I whispered, so that I could say I'd tried to locate her. Then I shuffled along the passageway to the forbidden zone.

Putting ear to wood, I could hear rustlings and rattlings, faint grunts and groans. Putting nose to wood, I could smell zoo.

A writer needs to experience everything. Someday my fiction might require a description of the kennel area of an animal clinic. Armed with this legitimate excuse, I opened the door.

On the other side was a big concrete-floored room lined with cages — much like a pet shop without the fish tanks. Business did not seem to be booming. There was one cocker puppy with a splinted front leg, and one sleeping

Siamese with no visible wounds.

The puppy greeted me with enthusiasm tinged with complaint, like a human patient yearning to check out of the hospital. His cage, I noticed, was clean. There was clear water in his bowl. Dr. H.'s business operation might be slow, but it apparently need not concern the SPCA.

While the pup continued to announce my intrusion, the cat remained obliviously sedated or dead. I was just leaning toward the latter's cage, hoping to see a telltale rise and fall of furry ribs, when Rosie strode into the room.

'Just what do you think you're doing?' she said.

One of the advantages to being old is you don't have to apologize for the dumb things you do. People expect and excuse your transgressions in the name of senility.

'Rosie. Is there a rest room around here?'

'You aren't allowed back here,' Rosie said. Though I couldn't see her eyebrows for her bangs, I got the impression they were frowning. 'You could have asked before you started wandering around. You have to get out — now.' And she muttered something else I didn't catch and wasn't sorry to have missed.

Here was an intimation of the Rosie I had known in school, whose quick temper and matching tongue had earned the sobriquet Rosie the Razor.

'Oh, all right, dear.' I obligingly shuffled toward the exit.

Before I reached it, there was commotion in the hall. A distant door banged, Dr. Hoffsteder shouted for Rosie, and Velma's voice quavered up the scale of a question.

Rosie and I rushed toward the summons, her indisputable lead primarily due to the sideways shove she gave me. She strode into Yappy's examining room, and just as I reached it, Velma stumbled out. The door slammed in our faces.

Spreading both empty arms, Velma keened, 'He killed him.'

The pit of my stomach contracted. What had I done to my friend and her little dog? Fumbling to grasp Velma's hands, I drew her into the open waiting area and helped her sit down.

'What happened?' I said.

She was squeezing my hands so hard, the arthritis sent shooting pains up to my elbows. I didn't try to ease away. I deserved it.

'He gave Yap the shot in his little leg and he was shivering like it was forty below and he pulled out the needle and he went rigid and went limp.'

It wasn't an easy eye-witness report to follow, but I caught the gist of it. 'Maybe Yappy fainted.'

'No, no, he's dead.' Velma's eyes were the raw red of tears on the way. 'He must have given him the wrong medicine.'

'Oh, Velma,' I sighed, hugging her to me, more ashamed of myself than the night I broke the jewelry store window. All my fault.

The telephone buzzed. Unanswered, it continued to intrude on our anxiety — a discreet, insistent summons. Finally it stopped, and there was no other sound, not even a clink, thump, or voice from the examining room. Before I could decide

I'd gone deaf, Velma began to snuffle, and then I wished that I had.

Perhaps ten minutes later, Rosie came out and walked straight to her counter/desk, not looking at us till she'd rummaged a big black binder from a drawer.

'I'm very sorry there was nothing we could do,' she said with as much feeling as a computer. She strolled over to us, flipping pages in the binder till she found the one she wanted. Spreading it open under Velma's reddened nose, Rosie said, 'Perhaps you'd care to choose a burial box. We have a cemetery behind Dad's house in the country. For a very reasonable sum, renewable yearly, your beloved pet can rest in the peace of your mind.'

'I'll show you a piece of my mind,' Velma snarled, knocking the book away and into my lap. 'You aren't going to touch my Yappy one more time. I want to take him home, right this minute.'

Rosie's step backward was her only concession to Velma's emotion. 'If you want to dispose of the body yourself, that's your prerogative. I can assure you, though, we can do it with a lot less muss and fuss.

You don't want to put it where it'll pollute the ground water, for instance.'

Holding Rosie's notebook in one hand, I grasped the back of Velma's seersucker jacket in the other, just in time to abort her launch. 'Let me smack her one, Tirzzy,' she pleaded, eyes welling afresh.

Just then Dr. Hoffsteder appeared, carefully closing the examining room door behind him. He wiped under his glasses with a bare thumb and forefinger.

'I'm truly sorry, Mrs. Newby. It was apparently a heart attack.'

'I want to take him to my Doctor Trum for a second opinion,' she declared.

'Certainly, if that's your wish. You did say the dog was getting along in years. These things happen. Let me put him in something for you.'

'Why didn't you take him to Wayne Trum in the first place?' Rosie's exasperation whined in her voice.

'I hope your malpractice insurance is paid up,' Velma ranted, shaking off my hand and following the veterinarian across the floor.

'Let me show you, Mrs. Quizenberry,'

Rosie said, sitting in the chair Velma had vacated. 'In case your friend changes her mind when she comes to her senses.' She reached to flop open the book in my lap. 'We have burial boxes in all price ranges — '

'I don't think — ' I glanced unwillingly at the glossy color photographs of a fox terrier laid out in a blue velvet-lined coffin. 'Uhh,' I said, surprise knocking the wind out of me.

The deceased lay on his side, limbs arranged as if he were leaping gladly into the afterlife. Tucked between the two front paws was one milky white and perfect calla lily.

8

We drove out to Dr. Trum's in miserable silence. Velma insisted on holding Yappy on her lap. Of course, it didn't seem like Yappy, but rather like a pair of boots, in the cardboard box Hoffsteder had provided. The one time I glanced over at her, her tears had dried and she was staring stony-faced out the windshield. I'd already told her how sorry I was — and at least four of those times out loud — so I bit my lip on the futility of saying it again.

'It's over the next rise,' Velma said, as if I wouldn't know where Trum lived.

We made the turn into his driveway, and she moaned. 'What am I going to tell Wayne Trum? Why did I take Yap to someone else when Wayne's been his vet since puppyhood?'

'Tell him the truth. That I talked you into it. Because I wanted to see the Hoffsteders up close in action. Because — because I'm thinking of getting a cat and I wanted to comparison shop for pet health care.'

Velma sniffed. 'Did you learn anything that will help you solve the murder?'

That was almost what Paul had asked me after we visited John Junior. Paul had actually used the words that Velma must be thinking — was it worth it?

'I'm not sure what it means yet,' I had to answer the same as I'd answered him. 'When you're feeling better, I'll tell you what I saw.'

★   ★   ★

'Without performing an autopsy, which I certainly wouldn't do, I have to agree with Dr. Hoffsteder,' Wayne Trum told Velma. 'Yap had some years on him, after all, and heart attacks hit oldsters of every species. You can be happy in the knowledge that it was quick, and that he was healthy up to the end.'

Velma nodded, a handful of Kleenex pressed to her mouth. 'Would you like me to take care of him for you? I have a nice, quiet spot in the orchard for that.'

159

Velma continued to nod, and Dr. Trum patted her shoulder as he herded her toward the door.

We were in what had once been a farm family kitchen — a big open room with warped oak floors and scarred white-painted cabinets. The south windows poured sunlight and a breeze inside.

'Dr. Trum, could I speak to you for a moment?' I said, hanging back from the screen door that he'd squeaked open for Velma. She went on out and picked her way across the shaggy side yard toward the Buick.

Trum looked at me the way a doctor does — politely caring with just a dash of worry. A man with the face and stature of a boy, he was wearing a blue plaid shirt with a rip in one sleeve, jeans on their last knees, and black gym shoes. He was the kind of vet you wished could treat you for your human maladies. Yappy should have spent his last moments in this man's hands. Not because the poor dog could have been saved, but because he couldn't be.

'Do you bury pets in boxes?' I came

briskly to the point.

'No. Generally what we do is cremate. And bury the ashes.'

'Is it unusual to bury pets in boxes?'

'Not at all. If the owner prefers.'

'If the dog were buried in a box, what would you put in the box? Besides the dog.'

Trum's forehead wrinkled momentarily. 'Toys. Perhaps a favorite dish. Whatever the pet's master or mistress wants.'

'One flower?'

'Certainly.'

'Routinely?'

'Some pet burial services might do that.'

'Thank you.'

'Welcome,' he said, as if my interrogation had made perfect sense.

I tottered after Velma, dreading the ride home. As soon as I had the motor running, I switched on the radio to fill the quiet. We listened to farm futures all the way back to town.

★ ★ ★

161

Any of the Hoffsteders could have done it.

They all had access to Fuzzy the weekend he expired. They all were accustomed to planting lilies along with the furry corpses.

I sat at my kitchen table, the heat of a coffee cup comforting between my hands, and considered giving up. How could I — an elderly woman with no authority — uncover the motives and opportunities of my suspects?

Oh, I could speculate till fare-thee-well. Dr. Hoffsteder, for instance. Perhaps he was supplying animals to labs, lying to customers that their pets had died and then selling the poor creatures for horrible experiments. Maybe he and Rosie were operating a kidnapping ring to procure victims. And Lisa had somehow found out and tried to blackmail Hoffsteder or Rosie or both.

Maybe — Maybe Cynthia Hoffsteder was overcome by a fit of matriarchy and killed to extract one of her sons — Jay Jay — from the clutches of soiled dove Lisa. Or perhaps it was John Senior that she was extracting. Lisa had, after all, many male friends, although it did seem unlikely she'd be interested in an old vet with a brow like black arborvitae.

Perhaps the entire Hoffsteder family, inspired by *Murder on the Orient Express*, had dispatched Lisa en masse.

My YOW text and notebook lay in the middle of the table, more evidence of failure. A week of trying, and I hadn't written one paragraph of an assignment worthy of a postage stamp. I hadn't even made the effort to deliver my typewriter to a serviceman for fumigation.

Tired of this shade of blue, I goaded myself up to make a banana pound cake to take to Velma.

★   ★   ★

I pressed the doorbell and stepped back, hugging the aromatic pan against my aproned middle. The waiting silence underscored that this was a house without a dog.

Velma's footsteps creaked and cracked the hall floorboards, and she materialized

163

behind the storm-door screen.

'Brought you a cake,' I said, as if she couldn't see it.

She pushed the door outward and extended her free hand. Thank you, Tirzzy.'

I balanced the cake pan on her arm and then the door fell shut between us.

'I left the oven on,' I lied, retreating before she could not invite me in.

Well, hell, I thought, bustling home. For all I knew, Lisa deserved what she got. Maybe if I were privy to the whole story, I'd root for the murderer. The damage was done; I couldn't bring back Lisa; it was none of my business. If Paul and his cronies couldn't sort out the killer, then that was their shortcoming, not mine.

My phone was ringing. By the time I'd climbed onto the back porch, it quit.

An answering machine would be nice. For all those times I'm too far off to answer. Like in the attic or the depths of the living-room sofa.

As I cleared up the debris from baking, my mood began to lighten too. No more sleuthing, I decided. No more pestering information out of strangers in my role of dotty geezeress.

I would sit down now and write a short story. About . . . About the time that Butch Deem hired on as a school bus driver and couldn't remember the route and the kids navigated him clear across the Ohio River into Kentucky.

The telephone rang. This time I nabbed it on the sixth ring. 'Hello, Tirzzy,' Paul McMorris said. 'I have good news.'

'I can certainly use some.'

'We've arrested the murderer of Lisa Norvell.

'My stars. Who is it?'

Being all prepared for the last name to be Hoffsteder, I failed to assimilate the answer he gave me. It sounded like 'Mickey Mouse.'

'Say that again?' I requested, screwing the receiver tighter to my ear.

'Mickey Foust. You recall my mentioning a drifter who was in the neighborhood shortly before you found Lisa. This is him. He.'

'I see. And what is it makes you think he did it?'

Obviously Paul couldn't hear the disapproval-bordering-on-sarcasm in my voice. He cheerfully answered the question. 'He was all the way to Indianapolis in the stolen Jeep. He ought to have been to Canada by now, and certainly not in his victim's vehicle, the dumb kid. He admits he was at the Linebarger place and even admits that he talked to Lisa, though so far he claims he didn't kill her. At least he was smart enough to get rid of the gun before we caught up with him His fingerprints do match prints we found on the cellar door. It's him, Tirzzy. You owe me dinner. Cabbage rolls would be fine.'

'I want to interview this young man.' I swiped an impatient finger around the dusty crevasses of the telephone base.

'What do you want to do that for?' I could hear that Paul wasn't smiling. 'It's over, Tirzzy. You were wrong. Give it up.'

'I was just about to. Now that you're all poised to send an innocent man to prison, I'll have to come out of retirement again.'

'Oh for — how can you be so sure he's innocent?'

'Well, I can't,' I enunciated slowly, as if Paul were as learning disadvantaged as he pretended. 'Not until you let me talk to Mickey Foust.'

★ ★ ★

'Mrs. Quizenberry is the one who discovered the body,' Paul said to Mickey Foust. 'Naturally, she feels most anxious that justice be served here.'

The three of us occupied a little closet of a room next door to Paul's office. It had no windows and no furniture. It looked like an out-of-order elevator.

Paul had dragged a folding chair into it for me. Mickey, his hands cuffed behind his back, leaned against the back wall, as casual as a commuter waiting for his floor.

'Could I speak to Mickey alone, please?' I said, clasping my hands in my lap. It was difficult to look cool when I could feel sweat tickling down the backs of my knees.

'That's not a good idea. This whole interview is a bad idea. If Mickey hadn't consented to it, you wouldn't be here at all.

'All right, Paul,' I gave in gracefully. 'You may stay. Please refrain from commenting until we're finished.'

He heaved an editorial sigh and backed into the doorway to light a cigar.

'Mickey, I'd appreciate it if you told me your story,' I said, trying to look him in the eye as he stared at his feet and shrugged. He reminded me of a multitude of boys who had occupied the back seats of my classes. Badly cut hair, bad complexion, eyes full of disinterest. 'Young man, how old are you?'

He sighed hard and tilted his head to glare at the ceiling. Obviously I reminded him of a multitude of past teachers. Twenty-four,' he said, dividing the 'four' into two syllables.

I could picture him running away from home, hitchhiking north, following lines of least resistance, month after month, to this inexorable cul-de-sac.

'How long have you been in Preble City?'

'Couple weeks.'

'Ever been here before?'

'Nope.'

'Ever heard of a family named Hoffst-eder?'

'Tirzzy,' Paul growled.

The boy looked from one of us to the other, suspicious and curious. He answered, I'm sure more from desire to annoy Paul than from a wish to cooperate with me. 'No.'

'Tell me about Lisa,' I said.

Again he huffed a put-upon sigh and shifted against the wall. 'I had me a sleeping bag in that old house. Camping out 'cause I didn't have money for anything else. And I'm inside sleeping off a bad quart of rose, and I wake up to this bang. So pretty soon I gets up and goes outside to pee. And there's this girl laying on the grass. Blood all over her.'

I turned to glare at Paul. 'You said he said he talked to her.'

Paul tapped cigar ash into his cupped palm. 'Keep listening.'

The boy was still talking, not waiting for me to pay attention.

' — see what was wrong with her.

There was a red Jeep in the driveway, so I goes to look at it. The keys was in the ignition and a red billfold was on the seat. Almost fifty bucks in there.' His eyes glazed over, dreaming on that money.

'Foust,' Paul prompted, 'what did you do about the woman?'

'Umm. I went back over there to see if — well, hell, to see if she was wearing a diamond ring or anything. And when I took a hold of her hand, she grabbed me back. Scared the crap out of me.' Mickey shook his head, remembering.

'She was alive,' I breathed. 'And she spoke to you?'

Nodding, he put a bit of soprano in his voice to mimic Lisa. ' "Gimme a doctor', she goes. 'Shot myself.' '

The boy seemed to think that was the end of the tale. He settled his shoulders against the wall and shut his eyes. I switched around to frown at Paul.

'Tell Mrs. Quizenberry the rest. What you did.'

'There ain't nothing left to tell. The woman went limp soon as she said these things. Dead, no doubt about it. So I dragged her over to the outside cellar stairs and laid her in.'

Why?' I demanded.

'You want me to leave her out in the weather for scavengers?' He sounded as shocked as I did.

'No, I want you to take her to a doctor. To the police.'

'Missus, she's dead. Beyond help, see? Way I figure, the money in her wallet is short pay for the nightmares I'm going to have over seeing all that blood.'

And now the sixty-four-thousand-dollar question that had been burning a hole in my mind for the last ten minutes: 'Mickey, why did you put the lily in her hand?'

Both he and Paul moved impatiently.

'I didn't,' Mickey said. 'She was holding this flower when I found her, and she kept hold of it all the way to the cellar steps. A death grip, like they say.'

Shaking my head didn't clear any confusion out. 'And what happened to the gun?'

Mickey's expression slid from boredom to resentment. He answered, each word

171

accented, like he was sick of being asked this particular question. 'I. Do. Not. Know. There weren't no gun.'

'Then how could she have shot herself?' I wondered with, I thought, perfect reasonableness.

'If you're so all-fired set on helping me out,' Mickey said, 'you find out how she done it.'

★ ★ ★

'We're still looking for the weapon,' Paul said.

He and I sat in his office, Mickey having been delivered back to his cell. I pictured the poor boy sitting on his cot, face in hands, in the tiny barred room I'd picked out for Jerry Joe. Still, that cot had to be more comfortable than this chair I occupied. Paul had surely never sat on it himself, or he'd be ashamed to offer it to guests.

Paul tipped back his own chair and chunk-chunked each loafer-shod foot on the desktop. 'If you want to risk another bet, I'd say he pawned it instead of dumping it in the handiest river. Which means we'll find it eventually.'

'But even if it has Mickey's fingerprints on it — which it probably won't — that doesn't mean he fired the shot,' I said. 'Give the poor boy the benefit of the doubt for a moment. Could Lisa have shot herself? Given the angle of entry and her handedness?'

'If she dropped the gun and it fired accidentally. But the trajectory was such, she'd have had to be leaning over it or falling on it for it to go straight through like that. Not likely. Huh-uh.'

The sun fingered my back through the old-fashioned double-hung window. It threw my shadow across my lap and onto the side of Paul's desk — a little black cloud in keeping with my mood.

'Mickey said 'a bang'. He heard one bang,' I said. 'I was under the impression there were more shots than that.'

Paul stretched to pick up a letter opener to play with, turning it end for end on the arm of his chair. 'What made you think so?'

'You said you'd keep the number of

173

shots a secret, to help verify a suspect's confession.'

He grinned. 'Yes. And the correct answer is, there was one, single wound.'

I felt a headache brewing. This Mickey Foust development on top of the Yappy disaster would command an industrial-strength painkiller.

I shook my head, feeling lost. 'Why'd she have the lily in her hand?'

'She was picking posies.' Paul spread his hands. 'Come on, Tirzzy. Aren't you relieved that the case is resolved?'

Squirming to my feet, I stamped them, only partly to restore circulation. 'Someone besides Mickey shot her and left her for dead. I can't let you railroad an innocent man.'

''Innocent' isn't the appropriate word for our Mr. Foust,' Paul said. 'His sleeping bag was full of girlie magazines and funny cigarettes.'

'That doesn't make him a taker of human life.' I hated arguing with Paul. Our friendship seemed to be a perpetual two-step, one forward and a smaller one back.

'Leave it alone, Tirzzy. We're still looking for the gun. The case isn't closed. Quite.'

I meshed my teeth against any rash promises and headed for the door. I wasn't paying off any cabbage-roll debts yet, either.

★　★　★

It had occurred to me that I shouldn't leave the accusatory note in my safe deposit box, now that I was less than certain Jerry Joe was the one who would be trying to murder me. Accordingly, instead of driving straight home, I stopped at the bank and went down the clanging metal steps to the basement lock box vault.

Miriam Shively guarded the grilled gate, a coffee mug in one hand and a paperback romance in the other. She looked up, eyes glazed from whatever scene I'd interrupted, and frowned before she smiled.

'Mrs. Quizenberry, you want in your box again?'

'Just for a moment, if you please.' I signed the logbook beside her pointing fingernail, which was sharpened and painted fresh blood-red. She stood and led me through the gate.

'Hot out, is it?' she small-talked, using a second key from the chain around her neck in tandem with my key.

I opened my mouth, but before the answer could reach it, my brain had shunted off on a side track. Since Lisa had been worried enough, like me, to buy herself a gun, could she also have written, like me, a note to be opened in the event of her death? Could there be such an incriminating note lying in some safety deposit box or a friend's bureau drawer? Surely she wouldn't have left it in her own house.

'Mrs. Quizenberry?' Miriam raised her voice, waking me to the box she was offering. 'You need a cubicle?'

'Please,' I answered, annoyed at her expression. *Senile old woman*, it said.

Just wait till I solve the murder and you read in the Inkling *about my brilliant insights*, I thought right back at her.

In the lavatory stall ambiance of my cubicle, I amended my written allegation: *I doubt that Lisa shot herself. I know that I won't shoot myself. If I should die in the near future, of causes the least bit doubtful, please thoroughly question the entire Hoffsteder clan. Paul McMorris, if you're reading this, hovering over your shoulder demanding restitution.*

I called to Miriam that I was finished. She returned my box to its pigeonhole in the wall and clanged the door shut after it. Letting me out the gate, she wished me the ubiquitous 'nice day.' If those words had any real power, we'd all live happily ever after.

Emerging from the bank, I wished I'd brought my typewriter along, to leave at the office supply a block away. Another day. I realized I was procrastinating about that little chore, undoubtedly because I dreaded the sales pitch the serviceman would make for a new electric machine with all the bells, whistles, horns, and castanets.

Pointing the Buick toward home, I considered more pleasant activities — such as how I'd drive to Broom Place tomorrow and somehow get into Lisa's mobile home. I intended to search for the note she might have written and to discover any clues that the police might have been too busy to recognize.

9

It turned out to be no problem at all getting into Lisa's mobile home. When I stopped the Buick in front of it Tuesday shortly before noon, the door was standing wide open. It was blocked by Lisa's brother and a woman one could spot as a real estate agent from a mile away — mostly because she sported a red blazer in this ninety-degree weather.

My first thought was that I'd arrived too late and all of Lisa's personal effects would be gone. However, as I crossed the ragged lawn, I could see that the cardboard boxes piled on it were empty, preparatory to the Clearing Out.

'Hello, Leon,' I called ahead, smiling so he wouldn't think I'd come because his paycheck had bounced. At least I hadn't yet heard that it had.

He gazed at me without recognition. Surely he didn't know so many elderly women that I'd been lost in the crowd.

The realtor also stared at me, her curiosity vying with her annoyance at being interrupted.

Placing me at last, Leon smiled lukewarmly. 'Something I can do for you?'

'Don't let me bother you — I see you're busy. I'll just go inside, out of this heat, till you have a moment to talk to me.'

Leon and the woman parted, letting me cross the threshold into a little kitchen that smelled of defrosted refrigerator and old gym shoes. Moving right along, I sat down in the adjacent living room, on a brown corduroy couch whose cushions had been rubbed raw by countless posteriors. The furnishings were early garage sale — maple and plastic accented by knickknacks. I don't mean to sound snide; it's an accurate description of a decor made more depressing by dust fuzzing every surface like a five o'clock shadow.

Leon came into the room and the realtor went out into the yard. I could see her through the open wedge of door, trying to pound her sign in the center of the lawn with the high heel of her shoe.

She might have experienced more luck if she'd left her foot in the shoe.

'So what did you want?' Leon wondered, jamming his hands into his jeans pockets.

'I'm still trying to find evidence of who killed Lisa. Would you allow me to look through her belongings, to see if there's anything to incriminate my suspect?' I added a very faint 's' to the last word, by way of maintaining honesty.

'The police already looked, lady. There's nothing here.'

'Were they men or women?'

'Uhh, men.'

'Well, there you are. Men frequently can't find their own clean socks in their own dresser drawers. It takes a woman to find clues to another woman's life and death. May I look around?'

Leon considered. 'I guess it's okay. I went through everything and nothing's valuable.'

I wasn't in a position to take offense at his tactlessness regarding my integrity. Smiling, I stood and returned to the kitchen to open the nearest drawer.

Flatware in a jumble. Second drawer — potholders and plastic bags in a jumble. I flashed another smile at Leon and drew out drawer number three. Kitchen tools, also in A.J.

The real estate lady came to the door to ask for a hammer. Leon opened drawer four and stirred up the very thing. The two of them exited, and I made straight for the bedroom area.

There were a pair of bedrooms. One had been delegated as a sewing room, the first indication of a Lisa activity I could wholly approve. Continuing on to the back bedroom, I tried not to look too closely at the disheveled bed, which was past needing to be changed and cried out for reclamation.

Anyway, here was my goal — a tiny drop-front desk. The pigeonholes inside were crammed with bills and advertisements. The little black book I exultantly seized upon turned out to be only a home budget record, and blank after the month of February, at that.

I dropped it to swoop upon another possible treasure. A checkbook! I skimmed down the entries. The checks had been written for groceries and other necessities — if you consider Video To Go a necessity. The deposits were regular and in amounts consistent with Lisa's tending bar for a living.

Disappointed, I put aside the checkbook and drew out the desk's little center drawer. Coupons. Rubber bands and paperclips. Postage stamps. Two photographs. One showed Lisa standing in front of this house trailer, and 'showed' was the right word, as she wore a bikini that could have passed through the eye of a darning needle. The other picture, blurred and grainy, depicted a weeks-old infant sagging like an under-watered house plant in his or her plastic carrier. I turned both pictures over, and of course the backs were blank — so few people take the time to label photos for the benefit of future generations.

This search was certainly not turning out to be a wildly exciting experience in danger of over-exerting my heart. Perhaps I'd underestimated the police. Perhaps they had found and confiscated the most promising memorabilia in Lisa's belongings.

Sighing, I turned to study the rest of the room. A bedside stand beckoned. The paraphernalia inside was rubber and cellophane and leather, and I swished the drawer shut before I could get too clear an idea of what it was.

That left the bureau drawers. I started with the easy, top, one. It was full of lacy undergarments, a froth of pastels and blacks. The middle drawer contained more practical wear — T-shirts and socks and, I'm sorry to say, two pairs of men's white briefs.

'Mrs. — Mrs.?' Leon called.

He'd said I could do this, but I feared he would change his mind. Pretending not to hear him, I hurried to the third and final drawer. It was the jumble to end all jumbles. My knees complained as I knelt to see better.

Music tapes. Income tax papers. Recipe clippings. Bill stubs.

I sifted the mess with both hands.

Greeting cards — none signed by Jay Jay. Business and personal letters. I fumbled through them, hearing Leon coming.

'Listen, I've been thinking — ' Leon said as he approached in the hallway, and I opened my handbag and stuffed the sheaf of letters inside.

The next layer of debris in the drawer was newspaper clippings, and I scooped them up and crammed them into my bag as well.

' — I don't think you ought to be involving yourself in this thing.' Leon stepped into the room and I pressed the purse against my stomach to close it. 'Like I said before, leave it to the cops. You could get hurt, you know.'

Using the open drawer as a brace, I pushed myself to a stand, palming an errant clipping in the process. Touched at his concern that I might be murdered, I was about to tell him so.

Leon overrode me. 'You fall down while you're here and I'm open to a law suit.'

'Oh. Yes, dear, I understand.' I placed one shoe on the center of the bureau drawer and pressed it shut. 'Well, then, I'll be going.'

He led me to the front door, giving me a chance, while his back was turned, to peek behind the framed ocean waves print in the narrow hall. I found nothing of interest to anyone except an arachnologist.

The realtor, having successfully planted her sign, now sat at the dinette table filling out forms. She glanced up to give me a preoccupied smile, too brief for me to return.

'Leon,' I said, 'let me give you my address and phone number, in case you come across anything that might help us.'

'Help us what?'

Tact is so often wasted on the young. 'You know. Your sister's unfortunate — her murder.'

He nodded, but without conviction.

I whipped out my trusty notebook and almost brought the precious news clippings with it. One did flutter free, but I bent to retrieve it as hastily as possible, and no one seemed to notice but me. I wrote the information on a blank sheet and ripped it out.

'Feel free to call me anytime,' I said,

handing it over. I could see from the lack of interest with which he took it that he would probably throw it away the first time he emptied his pockets.

I turned to go. Through the gaping front door wafted the screech-whap-clang of the neighboring children out to play. The breeze smelled of tar and fresh bread.

Thanking Leon, I stepped down to the concrete slab, thinking of how many times Lisa must have done exactly this — walked into the light and sound and scents of her next small or large adventure.

I hoped that she had noticed.

As I strolled toward my car, a fierce racket manifested itself, a motor far down the street and coming closer. By the time I reached the Buick, a silver and black motorcycle — a huge thing up close — nosed into the brown grass of Lisa's yard.

I stopped, not because the machine was in my way, but because I was momentarily blinded by the late sun mirrored in all that chrome. The noise cut off and quiet rushed back.

'Afternoon, ma'am,' a deep voice said, and the man responsible rose off the seat, into my vision. Rose and rose. Throwing a leg over the saddle, he booted the kick stand and stepped away, where I could get a better look.

Besides being very tall, he was very wide. His denim shirt must have been an extra-extra-large, while his faded blue jeans apparently didn't come in a size large enough. I mentally winced, imagining having to sit in a fit that tight. Most impressive, the rolled sleeves and open collar showed muscle, not flab. But I confess that most impressive of all, to an elderly white lady from a predominately white town, was his skin, the smooth, shiny, rich brown of an Ohio buckeye.

'Is Lisa home?' he rumbled, tucking his helmet under one arm.

Oh, dear. I glanced back at the mobile home, wishing Leon would come out. He wasn't in sight.

The man had shaved or lost his hair. Obviously thinking me hard of hearing, he asked again in a roar, 'Is Lisa home?'

'You've been out of town,' I hazarded.

'Yeah. How the devil did you know?' he continued, thoughtfully, to yell.

I peeped over my shoulder, but the bellowing had not drawn Leon to the front door. 'Lisa isn't home, but her brother is. Do you know Leon?'

'Oh, sure. Where's Lisa?'

I shook my key ring to free the Buick key, edging away. A man who uses 'ma'am' on strange old ladies is probably not going to shake them in a fit of rage when they deliver bad news. Still, to be on the safe side — 'Leon will tell you,' I said.

'Is something wrong?' One of his long arms reached out and he snagged my arm with his titanic fingers. It wasn't a painful grip, so I stood still for it, especially when I saw the honest concern in his black coffee eyes.

'Yes, I'm afraid something's very wrong, Mr. — '

'Call me Julian.'

'Julian, I have very bad news. Lisa is dead.'

He jerked back as if I'd punched him — if I could punch that hard. His warm hand dropped away from my sweaty arm.

He stared into my eyes while his own grew damp and damper. 'Dead?'

'Worse news, she was murdered.'

'Damn, oh damn.' It was the quietest thing he'd said. He shook his head as his face screwed up with grief.

Without hesitation, I stepped up to him and wrapped my arms around him as far as they would go. It was like hugging a hot refrigerator. 'I'm sorry. Was she a close friend?'

'Such a sweet kid. Who would want to hurt her?'

'No one knows. Yet.' I patted his ribs and backed away.

'When? Where? How?' He swiped at his nose with a fist, and I could see the anger beginning to crowd out the sorrow.

'Leon will tell you.' I hastened around the front of the Buick and fumbled my way in.

Julian had already paced to the front step; he ducked to go through the doorway. Being excruciatingly careful to pull straight out and not so much as tap the resplendent motorcycle, I headed toward home.

Of course, the first thing I wanted to do when I arrived safely home was sort through my stolen reading matter. But what I did do was check on Velma.

She wouldn't want to be checked upon. Therefore, I needed an excuse, a favor to ask, an item to borrow. Something that had nothing whatever to do with small dogs or anyone named Hoffsteder. Mention of the latter, I was sure, would have Velma reaching for her biggest club.

That was it. Club. The Garden Club would be meeting at Velma's house in the morning. I'd ask if she needed any extra chairs.

She answered my knock wearing an apron, her cheeks ruddy from whatever she'd been slaving over in the kitchen.

It smelled like spaghetti sauce. She came out instead of asking me in, and we gave each other the kind of smiles politicians exchange before the debate commences.

'I wondered if you needed any extra seating for the club meeting,' I said, setting one fist on a hip in a show of casualness.

'I don't believe so, Tirzzy. If I do, I'll let you know.' She wiped her hands on her apron and gazed at the street, where old Marion Waverly was puttering by on his riding lawn mower, his usual method of transportation since the state had revoked his driver's license for failing the eye test.

'Well, all right.' I hadn't thought to have a backup reason for being here, in case my extra-chair offer failed. 'You need anything else then? Glasses? Plates?'

'No, Tirzzy. Thank you.'

The sound of Waverly's motor faded. Deep inside Velma's house, the grandfather clock chimed three rich notes.

'I'll let you get back to what you were doing, then,' I said. 'Come over for coffee in the morning. I'll make crullers.'

'I better not promise. I got a lot to do to get ready by eleven o'clock.'

'Oh, sure.'

Her door slapped shut before I was halfway down the steps. I set out across the pair of driveways. Velma didn't shout after me to wait, come back.

* ★ ★

Upending my handbag on the kitchen table and weeding out my own belongings, I tidied up what was left into a semi-neat pile of Lisa's papers. Next I polished my bifocals with the hem of my dress. Then, having tantalized myself long enough, I picked up the first letter.

It was a sales pitch for a vacuum cleaner called Ka-broom. I began a discard pile.

The next letter touted diet pills. Illustrated by a before picture (overweight, overexposed female) and after picture (same woman in a sheath dress, holding her breath), it asked, 'Are you too much woman for any man?' Remembering Lisa's tiny physique, I wondered if Svelte Twice-a-Day had indeed worked miracles.

Letter three. A renewal notice for *Playgirl* which, I surmised from reading the list of coming attractions, had little to do with the theater.

My eagerness atrophied as the minutes ticked by and nothing pertinent to my investigation came to hand. The few personal notes were signed C. C. (an

invitation to 'hop a rattler to New York!')
or Wooster (what seemed to be a love
letter though it rambled peculiarly into
sports, asking about a score).

I sorted out and scanned all the letters,
and none of them began, 'To whom it
may concern: if I am murdered, the killer
is . . . '

The newspaper clippings seemed to be
from the *Cincinnati Enquirer* — cartoons, household and handyman hints, a
few recipes. I sifted through them
one-handed, the other fist propping my
chin, eyes beginning to glaze.

Here was a little article about — of all
things — having a miniature pig for a pet.
'Beauty of it is,' the writer wrote, 'when a
dog or cat dies, all you can do is bury it.'

My elbow slipped off the table top and
popped my eyelids open. Disgusted with
the time wasted, I scraped the clippings
together to put them into an envelope
with the letters. What written explanation
could I give when I mailed them back to
Leon — *These papers seemed to have
stuck to the bottom of my shoe?*

My fingers shook free one larger,

yellower scrap of newsprint. 'Darke County Fair,' the headline proclaimed. Darke County? My abdomen did a half gainer. My now alert eyes skipped to the top of the clipping. *The Greenville Advocate*, date cut off. Why the heck had Lisa kept an ad for a county fair? My fingers wisely turned the clipping over. The headline jumped up to meet me: 'One Hurt in Roll-over.'

'Ms. Lisa Norvell of Cincinnati is in critical condition today with head injuries at Darke County Hospital following a one-car accident on Red Fox Road. Officers called to the scene at shortly after midnight found Norvell's '85 Bronco on its top in the side ditch and Norvell, who was apparently not wearing a seat belt, unconscious in a nearby field.

'It is believed the Bronco was traveling at a high rate of speed shortly before the accident. A light rainfall earlier may have contributed to Norvell's losing control of her vehicle. No charges have been filed, pending continuing investigation.'

Fascinating. Perhaps irrelevant, but certainly deserving further study.

Was Red Fox Road anywhere near John Junior's farm? Some detective I, not to have noticed signposts. Paul had been both driver and navigator on our Sunday outing.

Scooting back my chair, I stood and poured myself some iced tea, and then, unable to think of a better plan, I dialed the police station and asked for Paul.

'Can I say who's calling?' the switchboard operator asked.

'I don't know, dear,' old habit made me answer. 'Have you tried?'

After a reasonably short wait, Paul said, 'It must be Tirzzy.'

'What's the name of the road that runs by John Junior's farm?' I asked straight out, not wanting to detain a busy man.

'If you want to be a stickler for accuracy, there're probably several roads that define his acreage.'

I could hear his chair cheep as he settled back to talk to me. I don't believe that's the position an irritated man takes. It made me relax some too.

'All right, Paul. Do you know the name of any of them?'

'Why do you want to know?'

'I think — ' What I thought was it was a mistake to tell him why I wanted to know. ' — Lisa Norvell crashed her automobile into one of his ditches a few years back.'

'Hmm.'

The refrigerator cycled off for a few minutes, and I rubbed my back against its comforting coolness, listening to Paul think.

'Well, Tirzzy, that would be a coincidence.'

'Do you recall any road names?'

'Wolf.'

'Wolf?'

'Maybe Wolverine.'

'Wolverine. What color?'

'What color? Uhh, Red. Red Fox.'

I smacked the counter with the flat of my free hand. 'A-ha!'

Paul groaned. 'Coincidences happen.'

'Thank you. I'll keep that in mind.'

'Wait, wait — what are you going to do?'

'Go to a morgue,' I said as happily as I felt.

★ ★ ★

Actually they aren't called morgues anymore. The euphemistic name, I believe, is 'newspaper reference library.'

Although I had already made quite a day of it, having already driven to Cincy and back, I was too eager to wait until Wednesday afternoon, which would be the next time I'd have free since the Garden Club meeting would tie up my morning. And so, shortly after hanging up on Paul, I set out for Greenville.

There was no use inviting Velma to go along. If she's too busy for crullers, she's certainly too busy for car trips.

★ ★ ★

I took the less scenic route, though even US 127 has its bright spots. At the edge of town, I stopped at a convenience store to ask directions to the newspaper office. The male cashier, whose mobile mouth reminded me of a number sixty-four rubber band, said *The Advocate* was located at North Main and Sycamore, and sure enough it was.

In no time, I was sitting at a microfilm

reader, my face parallel with the ceiling as I tried to focus old news through my bifocals. The negative images and words scrolled from bottom to top in response to my fingers on the knob, or at least that was the theory. There seemed to be some delay between my execution and the machine's response. We jumped like a standard transmission car in the grip of an automatic transmission driver.

What I needed to check was August, county fair time, beginning last year. Since one roll of microfilm was the equivalent of one year of *Advocates*, each roll contained just one August, and then I had to rewind that spool, put it away, and thread on a different year's film. After performing this operation only three times, I couldn't help being glad that Lisa's youth, assuming she obtained her license at sixteen, meant I had no more than five spools to go.

But the fourth time was the charm. There under my jutting chin was the same terse story of Lisa's auto accident as the clipping in my purse. I jerked the print down to confirm the date. August 17, 1987. Almost three years ago.

Forgetting to be aggravated with the touchy reader controls, I scanned forward through August, watching for an announcement of Lisa's condition or an official cause of the accident. If any such coverage existed, I missed it, no doubt due to the angle of my neck cutting off the flow of blood to my brain.

I thanked the young mortician, or librarian as she probably preferred to be called, and left my microfilm mess for her experienced hands to tidy up.

★　★　★

Disappointed that my secondary source had proved less than informative, I drove back to the convenience store to ask for more directions, to a primary source this time.

'Red Fox Road, huh?' my mobile-mouthed scout said, considering.

Not wanting to beg more advice or use the ladies' room without contributing a little revenue to his till, I bought a plastic cup of iced soft drink. I sipped it, thinking that it should have been billed instead as soft-drinked ice, and waited for a decision on how to reach Red Fox Road.

'You go south on 127 to 49. East on 49 to I think it's County 14, and then north on that to I think it's Pinter Road, and then let's see — '

I wrote it down dutifully on the back of an old grocery list I had in my purse, not believing a word of it, disappointed that my guide was, after all, a one-trick pony. Then I climbed into the Buick and just as dutifully followed every twist and turn — straight to John Junior's gravel lane.

I slowed just short of turning in and studied the landscape. There was an empty look about it — no trucks or farm machinery in the barnyard, all the windows and doors of the house closed and blank. No one came to the open door of the barn to check on the two dogs sounding their alarms.

I eased on up the road, past the mailbox with its door hanging down like a tongue from an empty mouth. Nailed to its post was a scrap of brown corrugated cardboard: *Fresh Eggs*. A meadowlark in the waving green side ditch piped his familiar song.

As I puttered along, a chrome-tanked milk truck whooshed past me and yanked around a curve in the road; he was going to be surprised when he got to the dairy and found he'd churned butter. The curve turned out to be a dogleg that jogged over a noisy plank bridge and climbed up a moderate hill. At the top on the left, surely enjoying a sweeping view of John Junior's fields, stood a white stone cottage.

Impulsively, I swung the Buick over into the brief driveway and stopped in front of the grapevine-festooned porch. An orange kitten, tail fat with surprise, dived through a fault in the rock foundation. Shutting off the engine, I listened for baying dogs and heard only the whistle of air through my unlatched vent window.

Prying myself out of the car, I shaded my eyes to survey the way I'd come. The little bridge, deep in its hollow, wasn't visible, and a wooded rise obscured John Junior's buildings. What could be seen were acres of pink clover, teal-blue ponds, green cornfields. Here and there, barns or houses glinted, like buttons holding together the patchwork fabric.

'Help you?' an alto voice asked.

I turned around. The woman standing on the porch could have doubled for the witch in Disney's *Snow White*. Her long white hair stirred in the breeze; her misshapen nose overshadowed her toothless mouth. She even had the dowager hump and the wart.

'Hello,' I sang out over-heartily to make up for the start she'd given me. 'Sorry to bother you. I'm looking for John Hoffsteder.'

'That way.' She pointed.

I found myself staring at her instead of in the direction she was pointing and hastily twisted to sight up the road. 'Oh, uh-huh. That is, I know where they live, but they don't seem to be at home.'

'Probably in the fields somewhere. Maybe gone to town for sumpin'.'

At least the woman wasn't wearing black. She had on a flowered housedress under a spanking white apron, and a pair of thong sandals on her spanking white feet. I stepped closer the porch so we

203

wouldn't have to keep shouting.

'Perhaps you could help me. I had a few questions about an automobile accident that happened a few years ago somewhere along here.'

The woman swiped her tongue around her lips, like a cat when dinner's over. 'They was some youngsters ran off the road last spring, didn't make the curve down by the bridge.'

'No, this was longer ago. Three years in August.'

The woman shut one eye and studied me with the other one. Then she backed into the porch and, two-eyed, dragged forward a slat-backed old rocking chair that was missing one slat and some of its moss-green paint.

'Le's sit. I got bad knees. Can't stand to stand more 'n a minute.' She reached for another rocker, this one white wicker with the seat and arms worn to black.

'Thank you.' I told myself not to rush the porch and give away my eagerness for this tête-à-tête — as if rushing porches was a viable option for me anymore.

10

I settled into the first chair, and it and the floor began to creak — it's impossible to sit in a rocker and not start it up. 'I'm Tirzzy Quizenberry.' I reached out my right hand.

She fumbled to grasp it with her left, squeezing instead of shaking it. 'Nellie Shilling.' Grunting, she dropped into the wicker chair.

'What a wonderful view. Have you lived here long?'

'It was my husband's father's place. Joseph and me were married in 1940, me just out of high school, and we moved in with his folks. His mother wasn't well, so I took care of her and the household and, top of that, we had twins — two sets of twins, can you feature that? Well, of course Joseph's mother had died by the time the second go-round came along, but still it wasn't no picnic for me . . . '

I'd loosed a talker and a half. While she

droned on, I horrified myself by figuring up her age to be about the same as mine. This poor old crone had lived a hard life, indeed. It wouldn't hurt me to sit here with my face in the shade and my feet in the sun, listening to her catharsis — especially since I'd be taking advantage of her shortly, asking selfish questions that were my reason for cultivating her company in the first place.

' . . . 1950, I think it was. Well, that was fine by me because — you want some coffee?'

'No. No, thank you. May I ask you about the auto accident three years ago?' I hastened to say, one word edgewise having squeezed an opening for two entire sentences.

'That would be the smash where the girl missed her turn and ended upside turvy on the far side of the creek.'

'Her name was Lisa Norvell.'

Nellie shrugged and narrowed her eyes at something or nothing in the distance. Afraid she was about to change the subject, I asked, 'Where did it happen?'

'Where all the clobber-ups happen on

this road. Down by the bridge. Folks don't slow enough for the ziggy-zag, and whoopsy, there they go into the ditch.'

'John's ditch.'

She nodded.

'Nellie, were you at home that — night, was it?'

More nodding.

'Did you go down there?'

'I did. What with my nursing Miz Shilling all those years, I'm pretty handy with the first aid. Once when Richard and Robert, the first twins — '

'Excuse me, but were you able to help Lisa? She had a severe head injury, didn't she?'

'Oh, yes. Out like a lantern. We all thought she was dead.'

'We who? Was John there? And Bonita?'

'John was. Bonita wasn't home that night. I can't recollect where she'd gone to.'

Aha. Was Lisa in the neighborhood precisely because Bonita was away?

Nellie had not paused to let me catch up. ' . . . anywheres close. But John and his boy Darrell and me, we all heard the commotion and went to see could we scrape these newest fools off the roadway. By the time I got down there, John, he'd already called the sheriff, but course it took a while for help to come, us being out here in the boonies.' She slapped her forearm and muttered, 'Missed.'

'Darrell's wife was in an auto accident too, I believe. Do you know when and where that was?'

Nellie didn't seem to wonder why I was asking all these presumptuous questions. I'd have been happy to give her some polite excuse for my inquiries, but apparently nosiness itself was all the excuse she needed.

She squirmed deeper into her chair. 'Never met that gal, Darrell's wife. She was killed somewheres north, is the way I heard it. Up around Cleveland. Poor thing never got to know the baby she'd labored to bring forth just a few weeks prior.'

I'd been toying with the notion of a connection between Darrell's wife and Lisa and the wreck. Now I let that go and pressed on. 'Lisa was alone in the vehicle, and no one else was involved?'

Nellie's head bobbed in counterpoint with the rocking chair. 'Only herself to blame.'

'Did you ever hear, by any chance, why she was on this road? I mean, she lived clear off in Cincinnati, I think.'

Nellie's eyebrows pinched together as she considered. 'No, can't say I ever heard.'

Feeling as if a trumpet fanfare should precede the question I'd been building toward, I asked it. 'Do you think John or Darrell or Bonita knew Lisa?'

'Oh, no. At least the men didn't. Ever seen somebody with blood coming out their mouth and nose and ears? Not a pleasant sight, I can tell you. If they'd of known her, they'd of called her by name and been way more perturbed than they was.'

For a moment, I could see the Bronco upside down, headlight beams glittering with dust and flying insects, and Lisa limp in the underbrush, her bloody hair black in the moonlight. John plunging across the ditch, Darrell behind, their flashlights jittery and their jaws clamped on distaste for what they'd find.

Nellie probably had it right. They'd surely have said something if they had known the unconscious girl. Besides, John told Paul and me that he didn't know Lisa Norvell. Could it be that he really didn't remember the name of the accident victim he'd helped?

Nellie cleared her throat. 'Course afterwards, they was pretty thick.'

'Thick?' I said, still back at the scene of the accident therefore pretty thick myself.

'I know she come out at least three times to visit then thank them, I expect.' Nellie sniffed and folded her hands on her stomach. 'She never did come to thank me.'

My thoughts braked and I put them into reverse. 'Nellie! This is terribly important. Are you sure Lisa visited Hoffsteders? Three times?'

'Well, maybe not.' Her tongue came out to sweep around her mouth. 'I take that back. Don't quote me on that one. Law, sometimes I wonder if I'm fit to be out on my own . . . '

I slumped for a minute. Disappointment makes me tired.

Nellie chattered on . . . doctor about it, but he'll jest say I'm getting old. No. It was probably no more 'n twice I seen her, that Lisa, over to John's place.'

I stopped rocking and craned my neck to double-check that the line of scrubby evergreens was still between here and John's house. 'How'd you see Lisa with those trees in the way?'

She didn't seem to take offense at my doubting her. 'The first time, I's over getting eggs when here she comes in new red automobile. I almost didn't recognize her all cleaned up and her eyes open.'

'What did she say? What did John say?'

'Can't tell you that. I was driving out the lane with my egg purchase, and I didn't turn back to ease-drop on her Bonita, the only one around as I recall.'

'Uh-huh, uh-huh.' Enlightenment felt so close and yet so far. 'And what about the second time?'

'Same deal. I was leaving, she was coming. She didn't even nod at me. Course, she didn't know me from Adam, her being unconscious when I come to her aid that night. Still, when we crossed paths in John's lane, I smiled, and it wouldn't of hurt her to give a smile back. How'd she know I wasn't somebody important, the guvner's mother maybe, down in the country to pick me up some fresh hen fruit? Once I almost didn't nod at this gentleman in at Kroger's, and turns out, it was Raymond Burr, out here actoring in — '

'Nellie, how long ago were these Lisa sightings?'

She stroked her chin, one eye shut in concentration. 'First one maybe a month after the accident. Other time, oh, I'd say just two, three weeks ago.'

'Thank you,' I told her earnestly, gathering my legs under me to stand. 'I greatly appreciate your help.'

She twitched around to study me from under her black, wicked stepmother brows. 'You want some coffee now we've chatted our tongues dry?'

I didn't, but somehow it seemed churlish to refuse again. A little coffee might be nice. I needn't accept any apples.

When I drove past the Hoffsteder place thirty minutes later, I slowed at the mouth of the driveway. That touched off the dogs, who were probably cussing me for making them get up in the heat of the afternoon. There was a muddy blue pickup truck parked by the side porch door. It hadn't been there earlier.

I was tired. Still, it wouldn't take but a minute to buy a dozen eggs. As I pointed the Buick into the chute of driveway, Darrell Hoffsteder strode out of the house and hip-hopped down the steps toward his truck, a six-pack of something dangling from one hand, his face turned to study the Buick as he came. I could see the moment he recognized me. He threw the six-pack at the front seat and spat deliberately over his shoulder.

I thoughtlessly braked nose to nose with his truck.

'Hello,' I warbled out my side window, all proud and happy to be here. 'Who do I see about eggs?'

'Sold out,' he shouted, lifting his billed

213

cap and resettling it. His blond hair was sweat-plastered to his forehead in Julius Caesar waves.

'Oh dear, are you sure? Maybe Bonita can find me a spare half dozen. Is she here?'

'No.'

He opened the truck door, leaped into the driver's seat, and started the engine, revving it much harder and longer than necessary. When I didn't move out of the way fast enough, he threw his gear into reverse, shimmied backward in the rutted barn lot, and whipped forward around the Buick. He raised one hand in some farewell gesture as he turned left on the road without slowing.

It's a good thing my feelings are not easily hurt. Putting my own vehicle in a tight U, I circled the barnyard and turned left on the road myself.

The Ohio countryside dozed in the late afternoon sun. The side ditches, full of mustard and dandelions, bobbed in a breeze. Red-winged blackbirds and yellow-bibbed meadowlarks rested on fence posts. The hot road shimmered with mirages.

I would pass the time between here and home thinking what to write for poor Mr. Golden, waiting with bated breath out there in New Hampshire.

What if? the YOW text advocated.

What if, when skin sunburns and peels, the new skin grows in a different color?

What if Butch Deem decided to hijack an airliner, but in his excitement, he couldn't wait and hijacked the shuttle bus instead?

What if the road ended at the top of this rise, and the Buick and I dropped off the edge of the world?

What if —

I glanced up at the rear-view mirror and twitched with the surprise of finding it full of muddy chrome grill. Checking the side mirror, I could see the shape of a ball cap behind the light-streaked windshield of a blue pickup truck.

The Buick shuddered across rough pavement and crested the hill. I steered as far to the right as I could, to let Darrell by, the road being empty and straight ahead.

His horn bleated twice, as if I were

doing something stupid, as if it were my fault that his front bumper grazed close enough to my back bumper to exchange tar spots and dead insects. Young people today drive as if their lives don't depend upon it.

I couldn't move any farther right because of the trough of side ditch, inches from the edge of the road. Still, the darned fool seemed to think I could. He motioned with his right arm, hand-sweeping from in front of his face to the far right side of the truck cab — get off, get off.

I stuck my left arm out my window and motioned too — go around, go around.

He beeped again, his grill leering squarely into my rear window.

Losing my temper, I ground the heel of my hand into my horn, and it bawled like a calf who'd misplaced his mother.

A quarter mile ahead, the side ditch opened up into a grassy apron leading to a gate in a field. Letting up on the horn, I clamped both hands on the steering wheel and toed the brake three light, quick taps, to show I was considering slowing down. The truck fell back, and for a moment I was tempted to stomp on the accelerator and leave him in my dust. But accelerating to fifty miles an hour — the most I was willing to go — would not kick up much dust.

I bumped the Buick into the turn-out and braked, twisting around to frown at Darrell as he went by.

However, he didn't go by. The truck squeezed off the road beside the Buick, blocking my way. And it wasn't Darrell, but John Junior who jumped down from the cab and circled around the front of it.

For one weak second or two, I wished that my 3913 S and W double action were nestled, snug and warm, in my purse.

'You want a beer, Ms. Quizenberry?' John called, reaching through the passenger window of his truck and waiting for my answer.

It didn't seem likely that a man bent on murdering an old lady would offer her a last beer first. When I smiled, my lips felt like old newspaper cracking apart at the folds.

'No, thank you, John.'

He brought his hand back out, empty,

and trudged around to the far side of the Buick. Reaching through the open window, he pulled up the lock button, opened the door, and slid in beside me without so much as a 'Mother-may-I?'

'You were following me much too closely, John.'

'Sorry.' He lifted off his billed Farm Bureau cap to pat at his forehead with a red paisley handkerchief, which he folded carefully before returning to his hip pocket. 'We need to talk.'

I should have been delighted at the prospect. Since still a little frightened, a little angry, and more than a little tired, I couldn't work up the enthusiasm the opportunity called for. I picked up my purse and fanned at my neck.

'Hot day,' John said. 'Darrell and me are mending fences on the south perimeter. When he came back from getting the beer, he said you were at the house.'

'Eggs,' I said. It was too much effort to recite all the verses of the lie.

'You somehow some way got the notion I know something about that Norvell girl's murder.'

I shrugged.

'You're a stubborn woman, Ms. Quizenberry. You got this notion, you're not going to let it go till someone pries it out of your head.'

I propped my elbow on the arm rest and my chin on my hand, watching a hawk coast lazy turns against pure blue.

'I don't want you out here worrying Bonita with your questions and suspicions. If I tell you the whole story, I expect you to leave us alone. Understand?'

'I can't promise not to tell Paul McMorris, so don't incriminate yourself. I don't know the words to read you your Miranda rights.'

'I didn't kill Lisa Norvell. Darrell didn't kill her. Bonita didn't. My two dogs and all my chickens didn't.'

'You left out Heidi.'

'This is about Heidi. Just let me tell it my way, okay?' He stuck his head out his window and stared at the sky for a moment. 'Think it's going to rain?'

'John, 'your way' is to stall, the way you used to do when I called on you to diagram a sentence on the blackboard.

Now you find a verb and a subject and put them together with as many adjectives and adverbs as you desire.'

'There was this bad accident on the bridge west of my house three summers ago. A young woman lost control of her car and it rolled over in the ditch. She was in critical condition for a while.' He twisted to look me in the eye. 'It was Lisa Norvell.'

I nodded.

'You don't appear to be surprised,' he said, facing front again. He stretched his neck and scratched at the blond stubble that glistened there. 'Anyway, that night when Darrell and I dug her out of the cornfield where she'd buried herself, that was the first either of us ever heard of her, first we saw her. She was this stranger who needed help, was all.'

'Did Darrell's wife really die in a car accident?'

'He didn't have a wife. We made her up.'

'But — '

'I'm getting to that.' He fidgeted, studying his dirty fingernails, and I was back in the classroom, trying to pull answers like a dentist pulling teeth.

'It was the damnedest thing. The damnedest thing,' he breathed. 'The ambulance had come and taken her — this Lisa Norvell — away, so unconscious she looked like a goner. Then the sheriff's department, writing up their reports, tramping down what corn the Bronco hadn't already destroyed — they left, too. And the fire trucks that had come just in case, and a tow truck that flipped the wreckage over and took it away. All the colored lights and idling engines and confusion of men getting in each other's way. All of that had come and left, and the night was black and quiet again.'

I watched John's face, expecting to see it give away a lie when one came around.

'Darrell had started walking back to the house. And, I don't know why — I don't know why — but I decided to check the damage to the field. I had this flashlight, needed a new battery, weak as milk.'

If we were into lies yet, they didn't show. He stared into space, and I knew he was in a dark cornfield following an anemic torch.

'It was August, and the untouched corn was high as my head. And I hear this — this — noise. I don't know. Like a baby bird, maybe. And I shift the light that direction, into a corn row, and there's this what looks like a big rock on the ground. And I walk over, and the damned light is so useless that even when I'm standing over it, I don't know what I'm seeing. So I squat down and there I am, staring into two eyes. I blink, and they blink. And then I see that it's one of those pumpkin seats or whatever you call them — an infant carrier. With a baby strapped to it. Jesus Christ, a baby.'

I shook my head, feeling his wonder.

'So I pick up the seat, real careful not to jar it, in case the baby's been hurt. The kid begins to cry. Not like she's sick or injured or scared. Like maybe she's hungry, you know?'

I didn't know. I didn't know if John did know.

'I get her home, and, first things first, I hunt up a bottle and a nipple — way too big, because it's for calves — and we sterilize it and warm up some skim milk and feed the tike. She looks fine. No bruises or cuts. All her arms and legs work. As soon as her tummy's full, she goes to sleep.'

'How old is this baby?'

'Not very old. I'm guessing a month or less. Can you imagine? Her flying out of the Bronco, the seat landing right side up, no damage done?'

'What did the police say about it?'

'Here's where it gets a little sticky. I did telephone the hospital to check up on the kid's mother. I guessed it was her mother. Lisa Norvell. But she was in a coma. No use leaving any message about how her baby was okay. I was thinking that some sober-sided social worker would come take custody, put the child in a foster home till Lisa recovered. Well, hell, me and Bonita could provide a better environment than any foster home. Save the county some expense and red tape. We'd keep close tabs on the mother, so whenever she came out of her coma we could let her know her little girl was safe and sound.'

'You didn't know she was sound. You didn't take her to a doctor,' I protested.

'Sure, I did. After Bonita got home from visiting her sister. A couple days later.'

'John!'

'I know, I know. But it worked out fine. Let me finish what I was saying. See, Lisa stayed critical for the longest time. It looked like she might die, any day, and then I surely didn't want the world to know about her baby. Just that quick, I'd fallen head over heels in love with the little dickens.'

'Didn't you think that there might be a distraught father somewhere?'

'He wasn't coming around to the hospital. He wasn't reporting any lost infant to the police. Nobody was — no relatives or friends of Lisa's. The woman didn't seem to have anyone worried about her, let alone her missing baby. What does that tell you about the kind of home life the kid could look forward to?'

'So Darrell was never married and never had children. Heidi is Lisa's daughter. Didn't Lisa want her back?'

'The day I phoned the hospital and they said Lisa had regained consciousness, that was one of the worst days in my life. Two weeks we'd had Heidi, and giving her back to her mother would be like ripping my heart out with my bare hands. I had them transfer my call to Lisa's room. 'You don't know me, but I've been taking good care of your little one,' I says to her. 'My little one what?' she says. She didn't remember any baby! Well, I couldn't send Heidi back to a mother who didn't remember her. Maybe Lisa wasn't her mother after all. Maybe Lisa had kidnapped her or something. I had to keep Heidi safe with me and Bonita, at least until I was sure what was what.'

Pain lapped behind my eyes, threatening to fill my head. 'When did Lisa remember? What did she do?'

'A month or so after she got out of the hospital, she came to the farm. That was another worst day in my life, me thinking she was come to make me give Heidi up. But Lisa didn't want her. Can you imagine? Didn't want her baby. She said if we'd buy her a new car — her Bronco wasn't insured — we could keep her daughter. For a new Jeep — not even a Cadillac. The woman had no maternal instinct whatsoever.'

'Lucky for you,' I said, rubbing my forehead. 'Still, she came to visit now and then.'

I felt John look at me. His voice came out soft with amusement. 'Mrs. Q., Mrs. Q. You must be the witch everybody said you were. Yes. Every now and then, she'd stop in on the excuse of buying eggs, and she'd catch up on how Heidi was turning out. So I guess she wasn't such a bad mama after all.'

'She was blackmailing you.'

'Naw. We gave her money from time to time if she asked. She didn't ask very often. We had a good relationship, considering.' John wiped his mouth with the back of his hand like a drunk thinking of something wet. 'I got to get back to work. You going to leave me and my little family alone after this? You satisfied now that none of us murdered Lisa Norvell?'

'John, you've just made matters worse. Now I can see that you have a motive for killing her.'

'I do?' He looked genuinely befuddled. 'What is it?'

'So you wouldn't have to worry, ever again, about Lisa taking Heidi away from you.'

He stared through me, his face as blank as a barn door. Then he chuckled. 'You got me there. I never thought of that one.' Shoving down the door handle with his elbow, he climbed out of the Buick. Before slamming the door, he leaned inside to add, 'I didn't know her well enough to murder her. I truly didn't do it, Mrs. Quizenberry. You drive home careful, now. No tailgating, okay?'

11

It occurred to me, as I pushed open my back door and shuffled into my kitchen on my last two legs, so to speak, that I ought to cultivate the habit of locking the house when I leave it for more than a few hours. Puddles of dying afternoon filled the corners of the stuffy room. I wrested both windows up to let in a breeze and the clacking of a neighbor child's wagon from the front sidewalk.

I was too tired to search the house for lurking undesirables, too tired to be afraid. The one drop of energy left in my body was going to be spent on a phone call. Dipping into my purse, I brought up my notebook and licked my thumb three times before I pinched up the right page. I dialed and then leaned against the counter to wait.

He probably wouldn't be at home. I was too tired to be disappointed.

'Hello?'

'Leon Norvell?'

'Yeah. Who's this?'

'Tirzah Quizenberry. Leon, was your sister pregnant about three years ago?'

'Jeez, I don't know. I was in California three years ago.'

'And she never said anything about a baby?'

'If Lise had got herself knocked up, old Lise would have had an abortion. A kid would have cramped her style, you know?'

'I'm afraid I do. Did she ever have large, unexplained sums of money?'

'Not that I noticed. But then, she would've spent any windfalls soon as they blew down.'

'I suppose she wasn't the type to put aside savings for her old age.'

His laugh was sharp and brief. 'Yeah, she got that right, didn't she?' Leon hung up on me.

I forced myself to brew a cup of instant coffee and microwave a stale slab of cheese Danish. While I refueled, I stared across the double driveways toward Velma's darkening house. The little newspaper girl roller-skated past, slinging her wares at porches. Velma's paper hit her screen door with a whang and a thump. The noise should have brought Yappy, his pogo-stick legs sending his head high enough to clamor imprecations through the open screen. The silence weighed hard on my shoulders.

After a few minutes, Velma stepped out on her porch, stooped to retrieve the paper baton, and backed inside again. I sat in the gathering gloom and listened to the crickets grind their legs. When I finally worked up the enthusiasm to retire for the night, I disconnected the telephone so that Jerry Joe couldn't reprise my rude awakenings.

★　★　★

A good night's sleep made a new woman of me and I was the old Tirzzy again. The morning sky showed an irresolute mixture of iron gray and Alice blue that could jump either way. For Velma's sake, I hoped it jumped to the blue. She usually set a picnic table buffet on her backyard patio whenever she hosted the Garden

Club in clement weather. Then we would sit on mismatched chairs in the shade of the high-limbed maple trees, the lunch plates on our thighs gradually oozing south like glaciers on double knit meadows.

If it rained, we'd crowd into the living room and talk in polite screams.

I telephoned Velma to see if she needed any help.

'No, thank you, Tirzzy. I have everything under control here.'

A writer must be able to accept rejection.

To occupy the two hours before Velma would let me into her house with the rest of the ladies, I sat at the kitchen table and opened my YOW text. I really ought to take that typewriter to be serviced.

'In three paragraphs, describe one member of your family. Try to make your description so vivid, a stranger could pick him or her out of a police line-up.'

The last place my father would have been was a police line-up. Like Abraham Lincoln, he once walked some distance to restore an item to its rightful owner, in this case, my friend Mary's right lateral incisor, baby variety, which had come out during a pork chop supper at our house and been inadvertently left on a window sill. Dad delivered it to Mary two blocks away, in plenty of time for the tooth fairy's appointed rounds.

Clayton Emery Quince married Esther Alice Maxwell because, he liked to claim, she was the only eligible female who stood shorter than he. This was Mother's cue to repeat the family joke about cigars stunting his growth — how, like Mark Twain, he'd come into the world asking for a light. Dad was wiry and strong, and he had a teeth-baring smile that would have caused ladies to swoon at a bijou movie matinee.

My parents made their living retailing hardware. The name of the store was Quince Hardware, but we took pride in everyone calling it The Hardware Store, as in 'I'm going to The Hardware Store.' Another, newer, hardware store out on the east edge of Preble City could reasonably be considered The Hardware Store, too, but Quince's had been at the same Main Street location since Great

Grandfather Maynard Quince founded it, which made us *The* Hardware Store and everyone else *A* Hardware Store. A customer would walk into the long, narrow, dim, high-ceilinged room and say, 'I want *The Hoe.*' Not 'a hoe' — '*The Hoe.*' Dad was a cautious buyer. He stocked one of everything. When The Hoe sold, he'd buy one more. In 1940, a winter blizzard filled the town with twenty inches of snow, and it took a month for the sidewalks to slowly emerge, one household at a time, as The Shovels came in and went out.

Dad was a volunteer fireman, a bird watcher, and a lover of parades, and for his funeral . . .

Here I realized I was about to exceed my three-paragraph limit, and I hadn't yet mentioned Dad's hair or eye color.

The present rushed in around me — the refrigerator humming and jingling its shelves, the anemic sunlight resting against the window screens, the perspiration trapped behind my knees, the arguments of sparrows.

In that lovely setting, a terrible shame swept over me. What would my father think of my breaking a merchant's window — on purpose! I couldn't believe I had been so cavalier, so reckless, so selfish.

I fairly leaped out of my chair and hastened to my bedroom, where I went straight to the small walk-in closet. I fumbled about in the near-dark, breathing lily of the valley and a trace of mothballs, until I recognized the satin-padded hanger bearing my best lavender dress — the one I'd worn to my retirement party. I stuck a forefinger into the tear in the left shoulder pad and tickled out the hundred-dollar bill I'd stowed there for emergencies. Not letting myself give it a second thought, I stuck it into a blue-lined privacy envelope, which I addressed in big block printing to Jerome August (looking up the jewelry store's street number in the phone book). Then I marched myself to the mailbox on the corner two blocks away.

The moment the envelope went down the hatch, I worried that I hadn't put a stamp on it or that I had put my return address on it. I returned home much slower, promising myself — and Dad — to behave better from now on.

It was still too early to walk over to Velma's. No one else had arrived yet, not even Loreen Previn, who kept all her clocks five minutes fast, until she realized she was subconsciously allowing for that and moved them all to ten minutes fast, until she realized she was now allowing for that, and so on. Last I heard, while the rest of Ohio is on Eastern Time, she'd adjusted up to Atlantic Time.

I'd no sooner sat down to rest while I waited than the telephone rang, and I was pleased to find Paul McMorris on the other end.

'I thought you'd want to know that we've released Mickey Foust on five thousand dollars' bond.'

'Oh? Where did he get the money?'

'Somebody somewhere loves him. An uncle or something. Money order arrived first thing this morning.' An abrupt smack of thunder rattled my kitchen windows.

'Oh, dear.'

'Something wrong?'

'I'm afraid the Garden Club is going to have a pool-side luncheon today.'

'It sounds delightful.'

235

'Not when Velma doesn't have a pool,' I said, watching Loreen Previn screech her Cadillac to a rabbit stop in Velma's driveway and rush at the front door as if the conductor were hauling up his step.

★　★　★

When a dozen guests had entered Velma's house, I strolled over and let myself in. Already the decibel level was at the biddy chorus stage, creeping higher and shriller with each new arrival. We haven't any rules against men being members, but no man has ever lasted more than two meetings. My theory is, male ears are too sensitive to endure the high frequencies a roomful of elderly women can reach. To say nothing of the topics of conversation.

'The weatherman should give us our own forecast. Instead of the wind chill factor, we could have the hot flashes factor.'

'Sibling rivalry? They've always tried to out-do each other, and they will, right up to the day one of them commits suicide.'

'She wanted him in the worst way, and that's exactly how he was to live with — a

236

regular despot. She couldn't go to the bathroom without raising her hand for permission.'

Laughter erupted more and more frequently, like sweet, hot pudding boiling up. Velma let me stand beside her in the little group that was discussing dieting.

'Rudy says I'm a chain eater.'

'I love to eat and it shows.'

'I read somewhere that you can gain weight just by smelling food.'

'My uncle used to smell food — sniffed every bite before he put it in his mouth. Maybe that's why he weighed three hundred pounds.'

Thunder added to the cacophony. Velma flinched at the loudest reports, her teeth clenched in a congenial hostess smile.

Another group of women poured through the front door. Hallooing and waving, they fanned out to work the crowd, leaving one figure alone on the door mat. Fittingly, a robust thunderclap stunned everyone into momentary silence as Velma and I stared aghast at Rosie the Razor Hoffsteder.

Rosie, meanwhile, surveyed the darkening living room as if she'd inadvertently entered a lesbian bar. The corners of her mouth curled down, her dark brows sagged below her bangs, and her whole body drooped to match her face.

'Oohh,' squealed Loreen. 'Here's our new member. You all know Rosie Hoffsteder.' Loreen hurried over to grab Rosie's arm before Rosie could take evasive action.

The Garden Club, like Dracula, is always searching for new blood. Our median age is about sixty-five. We want to pass along our botanical expertise and zucchini recipes to a younger generation, but the younger generation refuses to accept the honor. Bringing a new member into the group is a coup that ranks with producing the first ripe tomato of the season.

Rosie didn't look like a plant-fancier to me, and her insensitivity at showing up at Velma's home so soon after Yappy's demise indicated she hadn't improved her social skills since high school.

Velma, on the other hand, had social skills down cold. 'Miss Hoffsteder, do you like your coffee with or without ground glass?'

No one else noticed. The American coffee ritual is as automatic as 'how are you?' followed by 'fine.' If 'fine' is replaced with 'so bad I'm thinking of falling on a hand grenade', the next part of the litany will invariably be, 'that's good — see you around.'

Not even Rosie, apparently, noticed Velma's wording. 'Black is okay.'

While the club settled down to hear the reading of last month's minutes, a smattering of rain arrived, scouting ahead of the storm, wetting the sidewalks to release summer's scent. Treasurer Ginny Farmer reported that our bank balance stood at eighty-three dollars and thirty-seven cents, and that it was Grace Bell's month to have the waffle iron we received for opening the account.

Mother Nature overturned a full cloud, and rain sheeted on the house and yard. I hoped my bedroom window was shut.

President Sylvia waited for the exclamations to die a natural death before proceeding. 'Next month's meeting is at my h — '

Ka-blam! We all jumped, mouthing exclamations. Every lamp in the room passed out.

'Did that hit the house?'

'I smell ozone. Do you smell ozone?'

'I've soiled your carpet, Velma.'

This last was Loreen, who'd merely spilled coffee. By the time we'd finished laughing our nervousness away, the storm had already rumbled eastward to browbeat someone else.

We hurried through the rest of the business meeting, partly because the room was too dark to read any notes, but mostly to get to the main event of lunch. Our guest speaker, accountant Madge Dunlap, would be challenged to keep us awake after dessert, her topic being 'how to actualize supernumerary homeowners' insurance using valuable-items floater additaments.' I doubted I was the only one who hoped the electricity stayed off long enough to discourage her from the full text.

'Drat,' I heard Velma say in the kitchen.

I pardoned myself through a soap-opera discussion group and past Bea, who was sharing grandbaby snapshots with a glassy-eyed Rosie. Reaching the kitchen arch, I found Velma, palms on hips, frowning at a mixer bowl full of cream.

'We can eat our gingerbread plain,' Sylvia was soothing her. 'Or maybe the power will come back on before we're ready for dessert.'

'I've got some frozen whipped topping at home,' I volunteered, happy at the prospect of saving Velma's day. 'Two nine-ounce containers, I think. I'll get them.'

Before Velma could reject the offer, I plowed back through the living room and out the screen door.

The rain had spent itself, leaving everything green and steamy. A pair of robins shared a puddle in Velma's sidewalk, happily splashing water at each other and chirping. To avoid scaring them, I skirted too close to the peony border and rainwater sprinkled my ankles.

I threaded my way among the cars that the Garden Club members had parked in my driveway as well as in Velma's. I could have walked a little faster, but it was pleasant away from the voices and perfumes and press of warm bodies. My house bided, silent and gray in the dregs of the storm. I labored up the few steps to the porch and opened my whiny kitchen door.

241

It was like coming into a dark theater from a less dark street. As my eyes adjusted, I found that this was a horror show. The blood was so real, I could smell it.

It smeared the glass of the oven door, the white of the adjacent cabinet, and the eggshell pattern of the linoleum floor. It especially smeared the face of Mickey Foust, who lay on his back beside an overturned chair. One of his eyes stared at the light fixture in the middle of the ceiling, as if he were fascinated by the shadowy shapes of deceased insects in it. The other eye was a ragged wink in the ruin of his face.

His arms sprawled wide and his hands clenched on nothing.

I knew I shouldn't touch anything, but I simply couldn't stay on my feet a moment longer. I hooked a shoe behind one of the chair legs — the chair farthest from Mickey — to haul it away from the table, and I sank down on the seat, fingers interlaced tightly against my chest. I cinched shut my eyes and tried not to moan out loud.

Taking six deep, deliberate breaths, I

talked myself into calming down. The room smelled awful, like an untended public restroom.

Myself again, I managed to stand without touching the table. I half turned toward the door, imagining my little kitchen full of big uniformed strangers, examining my personal belongings. At least there was no need for them to root through my YOW materials, which lay as I'd left them on the kitchen table. Careful not to step on any blood spots, I leaned to gather up the books and papers and, crushing them to my bosom, carried them to the Buick and dumped them into the back seat.

Then I picked my way back to Velma's, careful, again, not to intrude on the robins' joy, wishing that I could be as oblivious as they to the hideous side of life, man's inhumanity to man. I slipped into the house and through the crowd, feeling like a ghost, sapless and invisible.

'I need to use your phone, Velma,' I said.

'I'll put the topping in the refrigerator,' Sylvia said before she saw that I was empty-handed.

Velma studied me, puzzled by this

latest demonstration of my flakiness. The telephone cord was long enough that, after I dialed 911, I could walk into the pantry and draw the door shut. I half hoped Velma would follow me — in the old days, she would have. But she didn't push into the shelf-lined room to see what was going on, her annoyance with me obviously stronger than her curiosity. My heart sank as I downgraded her condition from angry to furious.

A woman's voice said I'd reached the police. Too late, I realized that I'd really wanted Paul McMorris's office.

'I really wanted Paul McMorris's office,' I said, trying to sound contrite about it.

'Is this an emergency?'

'Not exactly. I didn't, however, check for a pulse. He might still be alive. I guess we should treat it as an emergency, to be on the safe side.'

'Are you saying that someone is hurt?'

'He's beyond all pain, more likely.'

'Give me your name and address.'

I did. She asked for my date of birth too, which seemed wildly irrelevant at the moment. I was surprised and pleased to hear a siren begin to yowl several blocks away. Perhaps I'd been too hard on Paul's place of employment.

'Wait for the officer outside at the curb,' the dispatcher said.

'Could you also ask Detective McMorris to come over here?'

'I'll see if he's available.'

It was exactly what I'd been trying to do since we met, but I refrained from telling his colleague so.

★　★　★

Poor Madge never got to give her speech. She was pre-empted by the drama of Preble City's two police cars, one ambulance and one fire truck snarling traffic on the narrow street, their lights milling and their radios crackling with unintelligible shoptalk. Many of the Garden Club members stood on Velma's soggy lawn, consuming pasta and salad and unadorned gingerbread while eating up the excitement of Foust's misfortune.

I missed lunch that day. Actually I didn't miss it at all, not in the mood, under the circumstances, for marinara sauce. Paul arrived in one of the police cars, and he ensconced me in the Boston rocker in my own guest bedroom, out of the way of investigative activities. I was torn between being disappointed that I couldn't watch what was going on, and being grateful that I couldn't. Turning pages of the *National Geographic Magazine* that Paul thoughtfully brought me, I tried to imagine what had happened in the previously cozy haven of my kitchen. I was very much afraid the room would never be the same for me again.

'Are you all right, Tirzzy?' Paul asked, coming in from the hall, a white handkerchief in his hand.

'Yes, thank you. May I begin cleaning up soon?'

'You don't want to do that. There's a professional service I'll call for you. The cost is nothing compared to the peace of mind it will give you not to have to deal with the mess yourself. You ought to stay at a friend's house tonight, to give the cleaners a chance to return everything to normal.'

'There's no such thing as normal. The

time is out of joint.'

''Oh, cursed spite, that ever I was born to set it right'.' He smiled at me as wistfully as Hamlet might have smiled.

'It's your job, Paul, to set things right. Now that you know that Mickey Foust didn't shoot Lisa Norvell, you can get on with finding out who did.'

'How do I know Mickey didn't kill Lisa? Just because he's been shot himself doesn't mean he's innocent.'

'Oh, pooh — two murderers loose in little Preble City? Not likely.'

'Ahh. So you believe that whoever shot the one shot the other.'

'Don't you?'

'Well, it does appear as if the ammunition is the same. It seems Foust was head-shot twice with .9mm bullets. The killer left us the gun this time.' Paul held out his hand with the handkerchief and peeled the cloth away.

I leaned forward and considered the engine of destruction. The L-shaped gray metal looked unpleasantly familiar, except my Smith and Wesson didn't have rust on the barrel.

'That's Foust's blood, I think,' Paul said, noticing my grimace. 'The weapon was under his shoulder. He didn't shoot himself. Not twice anyway.'

'Paul, I would feel considerably better if you would let me go check that my gun is still in its proper place.'

'You have a pistol like this?' He looked at it startled, as if it had suddenly squirmed in his hand.

'A dead ringer. Excuse the choice of words.'

'Where is it?'

'In my bedside table drawer.' I planted my feet, ready to stand on them.

'I'll get it.' Paul was already out the door.

I felt inappropriately cheerful. At last Paul and I seemed to be diagramming the same complex sentence. Now then, with his help, I'd get somewhere with my investigation. I crossed my ankles and began to rock in earnest.

It seemed obvious to me that Mickey had witnessed too much on the day Lisa was killed, although he must not have realized that he possessed incriminating information. While Mickey resided in jail, he was safe. As soon as he left the haven of his cell, the killer followed him to my house and —

'Why did Mickey come to my house?' I said to Paul, who walked in from the hallway patting sweat from his neck with the handkerchief. I trusted the murder weapon was no longer in it.

'Foust was probably planning to con a senior lady out of her social security check. You'd been kind to him before.'

'Kindness is not synonymous with stupidity.'

'I never thought it was.'

Paul crossed the room and, apparently intimidated by the snowy expanse of woven cotton spread, perched on the very edge of the bed. Elbows on knees, he leaned toward me earnestly.

'Tirzzy, have you ever been given a Miranda warning? You have a right to remain silent, et cetera?'

12

'No, Paul, I never have been given Miranda rights.' I rocked forward and stopped, near enough to reach out and pat his hand, but I didn't. 'How does it go?'

'Your gun isn't in the night stand.'

I frowned. I didn't remember that part of the recitation in any of the TV cop shows.

'It looks like your Smith and Wesson killed Mickey Foust.'

'You don't think I shot him.' It wasn't a question. Paul was too intelligent to think such a ridiculous thing.

He shrugged. 'Your house. Your gun. You could have popped him before you went to your meeting.'

'And my motive?' I grinned, to show that I didn't mind playing this game.

'If you shot Lisa, and Foust witnessed it, he was probably trying to blackmail you.'

'And I shot Lisa because — '

'Because she found out you strangled the hamster and put flowers in his little casket all those years ago in homeroom. Or maybe she dangled one too many participles, and you just snapped. Come on, pack yourself an overnight bag and I'll deliver you wherever you say.'

I didn't want to say Velma's, but that would have been the logical place, back when we were buddies, and, since I was determined to act as if nothing had come between us until she forgot that something had, I said, 'Velma's. But you don't need to drive me over. I believe I can walk that far.'

Paul accompanied me to my bedroom. I was glad that my mother had instilled in me the virtue of making my bed every morning. We stopped at the threshold while Paul leaned in to speak to a young woman who was doing something to my closet door involving a spray can and clear adhesive tape. I was delighted to see her, not because I knew her — I didn't — but because I hadn't credited Preble City's police department with the enlightenment to hire females for any tasks more

251

demanding than filing.

'Are you about through?' Paul asked her.

She didn't look up, intent on blackening the doorknob with her spray. 'This is the last.'

'Did you do the nightstand drawer?'

She flashed him a superior grin and said nothing, which told me reams about their working relationship.

Tucking the spray can into her armpit to free both hands, she gently tamped a strip of tape on the knob and peeled off fingerprints, I presumed — undoubtedly mine. Then she spread the piece of tape onto a white index card, took a ballpoint pen from behind her ear and wrote something on the card. Turning toward us, she tipped her head to look past Paul and smile at me.

'I need to get your fingerprints, ma'am. So we can separate out any unknowns we find around your house.'

'I'd be delighted,' I said, and her eyes narrowed briefly, as if she suspected sarcasm.

'Mrs. Quizenberry is intrigued by

police work,' Paul said. 'It's too bad we don't have the means for administering a trace metal test.'

'What would that determine?' I asked, stepping into my own bedroom at the motioned invitation of the policewoman who'd made herself very much at home.

She opened up a metal box on my bureau top. 'Give me your left hand.'

'A gunpowder residue test would tell us if you'd discharged a firearm recently,' Paul said. 'A trace metal would tell us if you'd so much as held a firearm.'

'Then we should run the tests, to unequivocally clear me of suspicion.'

The policewoman rolled my fingers on the ink pad and thence onto an adjacent paper form. She printed all ten digits, and then she started over, filling another section of the paper. Having the hang of it now, I assumed the lead, and we soon had that page smudged to fair-thee-well.

Meanwhile, Paul was explaining that we couldn't test me for gun-handling, because the tests were too expensive. Some of them required equipment Preble City didn't have, and some tests weren't unequivocal and might give positive result all I'd done was change a baby's diapers.

I never did get this wild remark clarified, because Paul was hailed by someone in the kitchen, and he left us to our dirty work.

'Here, wipe your fingers on this,' the young woman said, offering a clean white rag from her tool box. 'I can't let you wash in the bathroom till I check the surfaces in there for latents. You can use the kitchen sink, though.'

'No, thank you, dear,' I said, picturing myself standing at that sink, lathering off a little pesky residue, while all around me lay the filth of Mickey Foust's demise.

She left me to pack my overnight bag, and by the time Paul returned, I had my next question ready. 'Why did the murderer put the gun under Mickey's shoulder?'

'Hmm. Why do you think?'

I shut my eyes, the better to see a shadowy figure raise the Smith and Wesson and fire twice. I found that Mick was sitting at my kitchen table at the time, and that he slowly oozed off my chair and onto my floor, where the killer had rather contemptuously tossed the gun seconds before.

Opening my eyes, I asked the new questions that occurred to me. 'How did the murderer know where I kept a gun? And why did Mickey hang around waiting for it to be fetched?'

'Everyone foolish enough to have a handgun keeps it in the bedroom, usually next to the bed. Maybe Foust had already found it while he was searching for loose change, and the killer took it away from Foust.'

I nodded, able to see it happening like that.

'May I escort you to your friend Velma's?' he suggested.

'I need my toothbrush first.'

While Paul went to get it, I had time to think about the reception I was bound to encounter on Velma's doorstep, now that I was to blame not only for Yappy, but for the total disruption of her carefully planned Garden Club meeting.

Velma did not seem surprised to find me standing at her front door with my overnight case in Paul's hand. She nodded at him and pushed the screen open.

'Call me in the morning, Tirzzy,' Paul said, taking his leave, and I felt like a kindergartner on the first day of school, being abandoned by all that was familiar. 'I'll know then if you can move home again.'

'You'll find plenty of disinfectant and cleanser and such under the kitchen sink.'

'We'll take care of it,' he said, waving and striding away.

'Well.' I breathed but hard. 'This is one way to get one's house cleaned.'

'You can have Marcia's bedroom,' Velma said.

'Thank you,' I said meekly, following her into the kitchen, where the smell of fresh coffee awoke my appetite.

She took a mug down from the lattice rack on the wall. Her collection included a mug in the shape of Ohio, one made of Plexiglas with shredded money inside, and one that undressed a muscular young man as the mug's liquid contents disappeared. Velma handed me my coffee.

Steam curled up from it like ectoplasm. The mug was white, inscribed on the side in gold letters — *Try not to make any dumb misteaks.*

Through the bay windows, I could see bright yellow plastic barrier ribbons bobbing gaily in the breeze, as if my house were decorated for a party rather than a funeral.

'I suppose you want to talk about it,' Velma said, sitting down at the kitchen table and opening a plastic bag of corn chips with her teeth.

'Oh, no. Huh-uh.' I reached across to help myself to a chip. 'Well, just one thing. Do you think Rosie could have stopped in and shot him before she came to the club meeting? Since it was on her way and all?'

'No. But if you want to railroad her, I'll help you.'

'How could Rosie — how could anyone creep into my house without being seen?'

'There were a gazillion cars parked all around both our houses. The bozo could have ducked low and sneaked fast.'

'Surely one of the ladies was looking

out the window and saw someone go into or come out of my house,' I persisted.

Velma shrugged. 'The police interviewed everybody. It'll come out, if anyone did.'

'I'm sorry I spoiled your meeting.' I sipped at the coffee, and, sure enough, the biting heat brought tears to my eyes.

Velma chewed, sipped, chewed. I nearly dropped my mug when she erupted into a fit of coughing, sputtering head-shaking — praise be — laughter.

'Can't you just hear the minutes?' she gasped. ' 'A delicious Italian luncheon was served, followed by interrogation of all members by the city police.' I'll never top this particular hostessing. No one will. This has to be the Garden Club meeting to end all meetings.'

I laughed with her. 'The meeting to die for,' I agreed.

'Tirzzy!'

Our mirth slowed and coasted to a stop. We drank our coffee, and I felt better, and I think she did, too.

* * *

Marcia's room occupied the dormer attic, a little girl's pink and ruffled snuggery with a pleasant cross breeze. The bed was narrower and softer than mine, but, detecting no peas under the mattress, I slept well and long.

I helped Velma prepare a generous breakfast of sausages, poached eggs, oatmeal, orange juice and toast, and I assumed most of the responsibility for eating it. I would have liked a fat golden waffle for dessert, but Velma wouldn't get custody of the waffle iron for another month or two.

While we were clearing off the dishes, a perky little white hatchback car scooted into my driveway and a perky little blonde woman hopped out. Lifting the rear door, she dragged out bottles and boxes and long-handled brushes and I don't know what-all. It took her three trips to lug everything onto the side porch. She dug a key from a rear pocket of her jeans and unlocked the windowed door, holding open the screened door with her hip.

'That little bit of fluff is going to clean up that disgusting mess?' Velma said, obviously scandalized that I'd allow such a thing. 'She should at least have an assistant with her. In case she faints.'

The woman returned to the car a fourth time and stood beside it dressing for war. She pulled on a yellow plastic jumpsuit, a pair of rubber boots, rubber gloves, and a surgical mask. Brandishing a roll of paper towels, she strode into the house.

'I'll go see if she has everything she needs,' I said, dusting toast crumbs from the table into my palm and then into the sink.

The same two robins, I'd bet, were taking a dust bath where yesterday's rain had dried on the driveway. One flew off when I came too close, but the other bravely continued his ablutions.

The cleaning lady had loosened the yellow crime scene tape from the porch pillar to step over it. It fluttered on my porch floor like something alive but seriously hurt. My stomach fluttered too, as I remembered the state of my kitchen.

I rapped at my own door and called hello as I opened it. The young woman stood beside the sink, fists on waist, taking stock of the job. She was older than she looked from a distance, forty maybe, with a broad face that accommodated her big brown eyes staring at me over the mask. Her expression said, *Well?*

'I'm the lady who lives here.' I got that much out and then the slaughterhouse stench hit me, and I had to clutch my throat and lean against the wall. 'You poor thing,' I wheezed.

'No, no, it's my job. I'm used to it. This helps.' She pointed to her face, but she didn't do anything so foolishly polite as to pull down the mask. 'Did you want something, Mrs. Quizenberry?'

'Just to make sure you didn't need anything.' My tearing eyes made out the label of a king-sized canister on my table: ExStink.

'Just a check when I'm through.'

'How much?' Poor, poor Mickey, to come down to this — a matter of hazardous waste disposal.

'It'll probably be about four hundred dollars.'

I nodded dizzily. She could have said

two, three, ten times that much and I would have thought it a bargain.

Snapping the wristbands of her gloves smartly, she added, 'Your homeowner's insurance might pay all or part of that.'

'Oh? Thank you for the information. I'll leave you to it, then,' I choked out before I fled.

About twenty minutes later, Velma and I spied out her window as an assistant arrived at the clean-up scene. A lanky long-haired man, he, too donned the spacesuit, boots, gloves, mask. He disappeared inside with a hammer in one hand and a crowbar in the other. I didn't want to know what either of those meant.

'What a way to make a living,' Velma said.

'It probably beats teaching public school nowadays,' I said, but I didn't really believe it.

* * *

In a surprisingly short two hours, they were finished, loading their cars with tools and supplies, stripping of the protective wear, chattering to one another as if it were just another day at the office. I waved at the young woman from Velma's porch.

'I'll mail you a bill,' she called before jumping into her vehicle as energetically as she had jumped out of it earlier.

'They've taken down the scene of the crime tape,' I said, gazing at my dear little house. 'I guess I can go home now.'

'You're supposed to call Paul first.'

Our rediscovered camaraderie of yesterday had backslid a notch. Velma was polite but distant, like a bed and breakfast manager who was eager to change the sheets for the next guest.

I called Paul.

'Would you like me to come over to make sure everything's to your satisfaction?' he offered.

'Yes, but you have better things to do. I'll phone in my complaints if there are any.'

'Two of your complaints will be the bullet holes in the wall above your range.'

'I'll stick artificial flowers in them. How is your case progressing?'

'We haven't located anyone who saw

Foust sneak in, but one of your neighbors did happen to see another party knocking at your kitchen door.'

'Wonderful! Who was it?'

'I believe the name is Kellerman. She lives directly across the street from you.'

'No, no. I mean, as if you didn't know, who was it knocking on my door?'

'That's not for public disclosure yet. I can tell you that we checked your registration against the murder weapon, and it isn't the same gun.'

'Oh, dear, now I'm confused.'

'The pistol we found on your kitchen floor is the gun Lisa Norvell bought for herself.'

'And that means that my twin to it is missing. The murderer must have stolen it. I want to file an official complaint.'

'You don't need to do that. We're already doing our best to find it, believe me.'

'Be sure to look over at you-know-who's. And if it isn't there, try you-know-who's immediate family. And another thing, you ought to check into who provided Mickey's bail bond. Maybe it was the killer, flushing Mickey out into the open

264

where he'd be a clear target.'

'I'm already working on that. Bond arrived as a money order issued by a post office in Cincinnati. You know, Tirzzy, for every unreasonable idea you have, you manage to come up with at least one reasonable one.'

''If you follow reason far enough, it always leads to conclusions that are contrary to reason.' Samuel Butler said that. If you follow unreasonableness far enough, it might lead to reason. I said that.'

'They all laughed at Christopher Columbus.'

'Exactly.'

'You can sail on home now, Tirzzy. I'll keep you posted.'

* * *

True to his word, Paul rapped on my kitchen door at six o'clock that evening, presumably to bring me news.

I had spent most of the day working in the yard, ostensibly because yesterday's moisture made weed-pulling easier. Actually, I didn't want to be inside the house, where violence's invisible wake still lapped against the walls.

'Hello,' Paul greeted me through the screen. 'Everything all right? Are the cabbage rolls ready yet?'

I swiped an ineffectual hand at my rat's-nest hair. 'Come in, come in. I was just trying to decide between Dairy King and Pizza Eatsa. After cleaning the real estate out from under my nails.'

'Your yard looks nice. You must be tired. How about if I sit on the stoop and read my newspaper while you freshen up, and then we'll share our wealth with the Heritage House?'

Five minutes before, I'd been seriously considering going to bed without any supper or shower. Now I hustled toward the bathroom as if my autumn legs had just been granted an Indian summer.

Within the hour, we were seated in a back room booth at the Heritage, iced tea at hand, our prime-rib dinners under construction in the kitchen. It felt so good, doing nothing, I didn't even feel like conversing.

Paul talked a potpourri of subjects

— about the pickup truck he was thinking of buying, about a friend of his who was making good money moving yachts wherever owners needed them moved, about reading in the newspaper about a bridge-naming contest in Colorado where the winning entry was 'Bob.'

Our food came and quickly went. Paul continued to entertain me, dredging up tales, now, from his police experiences — the bank robber who was mugged leaving the scene of the hold-up, the police sergeant who wrote poems to present to offenders, the police chaplain who cursed more fluently than a sailor's parrot, the felon awaiting arraignment who wandered into and burglarized the judge's chambers.

Lulled by the good food and better company, I would have dozed off and slid under the table without a ripple, but Paul roused me with the magic word.

' . . . Hoffsteder. Of course, it's not enough to bring any charges.'

'I'm sorry. Say that again?' I drizzled a bit of ice water on my napkin and dabbed it on each wrist.

'Rosie admits that she knocked at your door yesterday morning. She had the wrong address for the Garden Club meeting.'

Hadn't I suggested this very idea to Velma? 'All Rosie had to do was stand at the curb and listen. We were making enough noise to wake the — hearing disabled.'

'Yes, but it was thundering then. She claims that with all the parked cars, she wasn't sure which house contained the party.'

'And did Mickey answer the door?'

'No. No one answered, so she moved on to Velma's without entering yours, without noticing anything untoward.'

'Did you find any fingerprints that weren't mine?'

'Foust's were on the refrigerator door. Most of the other knobs and handles were wiped clean. So was the gun.'

I pictured Mickey, the perpetually hungry American male, checking out my refrigerator and being disappointed by its primary ingredients of a bowl of sourdough starter and a box of baking soda.

'By the way, ballistics confirms that

Foust and Lisa Norvell were shot by the same gun,' Paul said.

'You find my Smith and Wesson. Before it commits the next one.'

13

Friday mid-morning, Velma came over. It seemed like old times.

She brought her own full coffee mug — the shredded-money one — and today's *Preble City Inkling*.

'You're a celebrity,' she said, shoving the newspaper under my nose as I stood at the sink rinsing oak-leaf lettuce fresh from the garden.

Drying my hands by wiping them down my sides, I took the paper. It contained essentially the same information Paul had disclosed last night, though I doubted that the reporter had interviewed him, as I couldn't imagine Paul using the word 'dastardly'. I knew I had not been interviewed, and yet 'Ms. Quizenberry was horrified by her second gruesome find in less than two weeks,' and the whereabouts of my missing pistol 'is most worrying to the ex-schoolteacher.' Rosie had apparently told this reporter, 'I'm innocent,' but by now I'd lost faith in trustworthy news coverage.

'You should get yourself a guard dog,' Velma said.

This was the first time either of us had mentioned 'dog' in several days. It made me feel like a prudish kid, uncomfortable in the presence of a dirty word. I wasn't sure I could say it myself without mumbling.

'I don't want a . . . a dog, Velma. A goat, maybe. He could help me keep the grass mowed.' Having used the word once, I was cocky enough to try it again. 'You're the one who likes dogs.'

'I don't want another damn dog,' Velma said, snatching back her newspaper and beating a hasty retreat for home.

That day I found I could sit at the kitchen table and eat a meal without casting involuntary glances at all the cracks and crevices where there might be blood stains the cleaners had missed.

I considered shopping at the High Noon Gun Emporium for a replacement firearm, but I'd already spent my defense budget for this year, buying the first one.

What would be, would have to be, even if that meant my ceasing to be. A sense of humor costing nothing, I consoled myself with the old Italian proverb: the best way to get praise is to die.

★ ★ ★

I dug the Phillips screwdriver out of my kitchen junk drawer to perform my bimonthly chore of tightening the handle on my pantry door. Women living alone tend to become handy with tools, and some women actually enjoy it. I put home repairs in the same nuisance category as income-tax forms, self-service gas pumps, and mammograms.

As I tightened the screw as far as I could make it go, I heard a noise I'd heard before. It grew, and I felt an unpleasant roil of premonition. A motorcycle. I willed it to keep moving up the street, but my voodoo powers aren't what they used to be, and the motor growled to a stop at right about the end of my driveway.

I walked to the screen door and leaned

far enough sideways to see the front curb. Sure enough, there was a black and chrome monster parked slantwise on the street and a looming black shape climbing off of it.

He lifted off his helmet and planted it on the sissy bar. His outfit looked the same as two days ago, tight denim and black work boots. His stride ate up the driveway in about ten steps, and then he noticed me and windmilled both arms.

'Miz Tirzzy! Surprise!'

'It certainly is, Julian. How did you know where I live?'

He clumped onto the porch, smoothing the non-existent hair on the top of his shiny head. 'Leon gave me your name and address,' he said too loudly. 'Whoa!' He stepped backward one giant step.

'What's the matter?'

'No call to pull that on me.' He frowned. 'I come in peace.'

Bewildered, I looked down at my hand and the five-inch screwdriver in it. 'I'm fixing something.' It seemed pretty obvious to me.

'Where I come from, those things are

considered weapons.'

'Really.' I examined it with new eyes. It did look, suddenly, quite dangerous. Feeling newly empowered, I stood straighter and asked Julian, 'What did you want, young man?'

'Leon says you're trying to pin Lisa's murder on someone. I thought I might help.'

For a weak moment, I must admit, I imagined Julian turned loose on Jerry Joe or John Junior, intimidating the truth out of them. 'I don't think so, dear. But it's nice of you to offer.'

'See, I know most of Lisa's friends. Leon said you were interested in who they were. Maybe we pool what we know, we'd get somewhere.'

'Oh. Oh, that sounds like a good idea.' Before I could reconsider, I pushed the door wide to let him in.

He hesitated. 'I don't want you to think I'm an Angel. I'm no Angel.'

'So few of us are,' I said, not sure what heavenly hosts had to do with anything. 'I won't consider you an angel if you won't consider me hard of hearing. I'm sorry I gave you that impression when we met.'

'No problem,' Julian said, a few decibels quieter, and he shouldered inside. Past the crag of his elbow, I thought I saw Velma's kitchen curtain twitch.

'Where's whatever's busted?' He squinted around the room.

'It's just a loose screw on a door,' I said. 'Would you like a cup of coffee?'

'Naw. I'd take a glass of water though.'

Laying the screwdriver beside the sink, I let the cold tap run a moment, standing sideways talking the whole time, as an excuse not to turn my back to him. He seemed all right, but one can't be too careful around a stranger who could snap you in two with one hand. Meanwhile, he pulled out a chair to sit at the table. The latter creaked when he set his folded arms on it.

'I really don't suspect any of Lisa's Cincinnati friends,' I said. 'I'm convinced the murderer lives right here in Preble City. Do you happen to know someone she called Jay-Jay?'

His mouth flattened down like a punctured tire as he concentrated fiercely.

'Well, no. Only me.'

I set his water glass down too hard on the table and some splashed out. 'Your last name begins with a 'J'?'

'Julian Justus Jacoby. Oopsie, that's three J's. I guess I'm Jay-Jay-Jay.'

'No. You aren't the wretch I'm after.'

He looked about as much like a Van Dyke brother as I looked like Sophia Loren. Besides, any man who uses 'oopsie' in casual conversation can't be Jack the Ripper.

'You shouldn't involve yourself,' he scolded. 'Defenseless, gentle woman like you. You could get hurt. Why do you care about Lisa anyway? Did you know her?'

'No. I care about her for the same reason you seem to care about me.'

His forehead squeezed into painful thought, nearly eclipsing his eyes. Then it smoothed out. 'I get you. People helping people. That's nice.' He sipped at the water. 'So how can I help you nail this guy?'

'I appreciate the offer, but I don't think you can. If I think of something, I'll let you know.'

He stabbed a forefinger my direction.

'Do that. I mean it.' Swallowing the rest of the water in noisy gulps, he shoved back the chair and stood. 'Where's the door needs a screw?'

'The handle. Right there.' I waved vaguely. 'But I've already tightened it, thank you.'

'Lemme check.' He lumbered around the table to retrieve the screwdriver, and approached the pantry door with the air of a man in charge. When he twisted the screwdriver into the screw, I heard wood splinter. 'Oughta do it,' he said.

I felt certain the rest of the kitchen could fall into total shambles and decay, but that one handle on that one door would never be rent asunder.

'You take it easy,' Julian said, handing me the screwdriver, handle first. 'I'll try to keep an eye on you.'

'No, don't do that. You have your own life to live. In Cincinnati, is it?'

'Right. Apartment near the river.'

I couldn't help speculating on whether Lisa had ever lived there, too. I felt she could have done — probably had done — much, much worse.

'What do you do for a living, Julian?'

He hauled a battered black wallet from a rear pocket and extracted a business card from it to flourish into my hand. 'Here's my address and phone number. You call me anytime you need help.'

''Senior Trips of Ohio, Ltd.',' I read. 'What's this?'

'Charter bus trips for senior citizens. First you got to join the organization for fifty bucks a year, and then you sign up to go someplace — Las Vegas, Nashville, D.C. — and I drive you there. Course you have to pay for each trip you take, but we try to keep it reasonable. Just got back from Mall of the Americas, and Monday I got a busload going to Graceland.'

Squiring a bunch of old, undoubtedly white people around the country was not what I'd have guessed for What's Julian's Line. I was most favorably impressed.

'Want to join?' he asked.

'No, but it sounds lovely.'

'I figured. You're too far from Cincy.' He winked as he pushed open the screen door. 'Or maybe you hate the group's acronym.'

As he swung down the driveway to his motorcycle, I had to work out what he meant. Senior Trips of Ohio Ltd. did seem an unfortunate string of words.

That evening's sunset smeared the sky like rhubarb on a pewter pie plate. Maybe that's why I felt oddly serene.

★　★　★

Saturday morning I slept late, until almost eight o'clock. Saturday afternoon, I drove to the Tisket Tasket. I needed only a few items, but I wrestled free a cart from the nested line-up rather than take a handled basket. One can lean on a cart.

The Tisket Tasket vestibule needed a helicopter reporter. No traffic engineer has ever been consulted about the ins and outs, and it is always every customer for himself — another reason to eschew a plastic basket in favor of a heavy wire cart. As usual, the music flowing out of overhead speakers was less catchy than the treble beep of bar codes at five check-out stands. Air blew down from the ceiling, chilly, yet smelling of hot bread. A miniature version of Butch Deem — all blond curls and angelic eyes — appeared to be hot-wiring the kiddy space rocket, which, if he succeeded, would play *Ride of the Valkyries* and chum him for two full minutes.

It being my turn to ebb into the market proper, I wheeled left toward produce. Choosing half a dozen beautiful nectarines and three passable lemons, I moved on to vegetables. The broccoflower tempted me, but it was a dollar ninety-nine a pound. It's usually too dear. If broccoli is seventy-nine cents a pound and cauliflower is ninety-nine cents a pound, shouldn't broccoflower be eighty-nine cents a pound?

'Tirzzy! Isn't it awful?' Loreen swooped her cart in front of mine and leaned across it confidentially, without lowering her voice one degree. 'We just saw her a couple days ago.'

My heart sank. That's a cliché, but there's no better description for the sudden dread that comes seconds before full comprehension. Which of my old friends had died in her sleep?

Loreen prattled on as if she assumed

I'd already heard the news, but her eyes watched for my reaction, and any demonstrable mystification on my part would release the floodgates on the story she was avid to spill.

How could I deny her that pleasure? 'Loreen, I don't know what you're talking about.'

'Rosie Hoffsteder! She killed herself last night.'

'Oh, dear.' I needed to sit down. Instead I leaned heavily on the produce counter and hoped it wasn't time for the cold geyser of the automatic sprinkler.

'I guess her mother found her this morning,' Loreen continued. 'Rosie had an apartment in that new building on Seventh. The Upper Anns. She and Cynthia were going shopping this morning, and when she didn't answer the door, Cynthia got the manager to open it, and they found Rosie in bed, overdosed on heartworm pills, which, of course, she had no trouble getting at work. But why would she want to swallow those when there are plenty of people medicines she could have — '

'What was she holding?'

'Uh — holding?'

'Did she have something in her hands?'

'The note, maybe. She left a note.'

'And this note is supposed to have been written by Rosie before her death? Taking responsibility for it?'

'Well, I didn't see the note myself, but I had it on good authority. See, the manager at the building is Hester Bonneville, and her husband works with my son — '

'I'm not questioning the veracity of your report, I'm just inquiring. And no mention was made of any flowers in the room?'

Loreen inched her cart away, preparatory to finding another more tractable recipient for her news. 'The note said Rosie murdered those two young people.'

'Did it say why?'

Here Loreen maneuvered her cart parallel with mine so that she could put her face close to my ear and stage-whisper. 'The three of them were a love triangle, only it wasn't the two women wanting the same man, if you get my meaning.'

I didn't, but I didn't want any more

gossip. I wanted facts, which Paul would share in due time. To get rid of Loreen, I nodded wisely, shook my head sadly, and bumped our wheels apart rudely.

'I have to go,' I said. When one is my age, that is often the case, and a peer will understand perfectly — no pun intended.

Before leaving produce, life being short, I selected a head of broccoflower. Then I homed in on the meat counter, where I exacerbated my extravagance by choosing a small T-bone steak. After all, in my next life, I might be a vegetarian.

★ ★ ★

'I'm pretty busy right now, Tirzzy,' Paul said when I reached him on the telephone.

'I knew you would be. I just don't want you wasting your time haring off down one road of inquiry while the truth slips away on another.'

His sigh was noisier than was necessary to exhale a mouthful of cigar smoke. 'You've heard about Rosie and you don't think she killed herself.'

'I don't know what to think yet. Tell me about the note.'

'I'll tell you about the note because I want you to concede that I have no more need of your sleuthing services. It appears to be her handwriting on a confession to murder. She shot Lisa because Lisa spurned her sexual advances, and then she shot Foust because he was Lisa's real love interest, who happened to witness the murder. Apparently he wanted hush money. So you were right, Tirzzy, about the perpetrator being a Hoffsteder. Now you can forget the whole thing and go back to doing whatever you were doing before you began discovering bodies.'

'And she got that stuff, the poison, from work. From her father's clinic.'

'No question, I'd say.'

Rosie must have killed herself. How would a murderer force all those heartworm pills down her throat? Still, suicide didn't feel right to me.

'It doesn't feel right to me,' I fretted out loud. 'Does it feel right to you?' Through the kitchen window, I watched the mailman pass me by in his pith helmet, blue walking shorts, and black shoes and socks.

'Of course, we won't close the case until we're satisfied that all the circumstances indicate suicide. You relax and leave it to us.'

Now here came another stranger, the UPS man, dressed in mud-brown to match his truck, striding a package up a neighbor's sidewalk.

I selfishly considered that, if Rosie's confession held up, my life would return to normal, a condition as exciting as a traffic jam. 'Did you find my Smith and Wesson?'

'Matter of fact, yes. It was behind a stack of magazines in Rosie's bookshelf headboard. You can have the thing back, once we're sure it won't be needed as evidence.'

Visitors come in threes. The third to invade the neighborhood announced himself half a block away by tootling a depressingly cheerful version of *Small World* on a recorded calliope.

'Paul, it's been nice talking to you, but I have to get busy,' I said, already sorting through my purse, which was yawning on the table. 'Do keep in touch.'

When I hung up the receiver, I double-checked the change in my hand. One never outgrows one's need for the ice-cream vendor.

The red, white and blue truck strolled up our street, sucking children from their play. I stood at the curb in the shade of my maples, examining a fallen leaf for tar spot, which of course couldn't be sprayed for this late in the year, so I'd be better off not knowing we had it. This one leaf seemed okay, aside from the fact it had lost its grip.

'Ice cream is fattening, Tirzzy,' Mona Kellerman called from across the street.

'I notice you have your money clutched in your hand too.' I walked across the asphalt. 'Remember when this was a dime?'

'No.'

She probably didn't. She and her husband were in their fifties. They probably hadn't walked five miles uphill to school in blizzards, or any of that good-old-days stuff.

'Tirzzy, I wanted to tell you, if you ever need help, especially at night, just give us a call. I keep thinking how awful it must have been for you, finding that young man.'

'Thank you. I guess you've heard about Rosie's death.'

Mona nodded. 'Poor girl.'

'When you saw her at my house Wednesday, was she going in or coming out?'

'Oh, neither. She was just knocking. I watched her until she turned away, and then I went upstairs to check which windows were open, and no one was on your porch when I looked out the next window. She must have turned around and gone inside while I was on the stairs.'

'You never saw Mickey Foust? Or anyone else?' I raise my voice as the pied ice cream truck piped toward us at a slow coast.

Mona shook her head. 'Just you, after the rain stopped. Putting something in your car.'

For a moment, I felt guilty as heck. Moving my YOW materials away from the scene of the crime couldn't be called withholding evidence, but Paul would certainly be irritated with me if he knew about it. What's more, the books and papers still resided in the Buick's back seat, because I hadn't felt the urge to write anything for three entire days.

The calliope died in mid-stanza, and an athletic-looking young woman wearing a red and white striped jumpsuit vaulted out of the cab. The job would require some athleticism, getting in and out of the vehicle all day — plus a strong tolerance for hearing *Small World* without end.

'What'll it be, ladies?'

'Blue moon,' Mona spoke up.

Forgetting the chocolate ripple I'd been planning, I blurted, 'A frozen daiquiri.'

I don't know why I said that, considering that I'm a teetotaler and chocolate is always my first flavor choice. When the two women laughed, I took credit for a good joke and amended my order to rocky road.

'See you,' Mona called as I walked home to retrieve my covert writing from the subrosa seat of my automobile.

It wasn't easy, carrying a drippy ice cream cone and an unruly stack of papers and books up my porch steps and through the screen door. I managed it without dropping anything until I reached the table, and then I bent over to dump the writing materials and shake the cramp from my elbow.

I would finish my ice cream, use the bathroom, sharpen my pencils, perhaps file my nails, and then I'd write something. Compulsively, I tidied up the textbook and the genuine buckram binder, opening the latter to straighten a few papers that were leaking out the edges.

Stopping abruptly, tongue to cone, I stared transfixed at the top page.

A woman knows the color of old blood. I'd been writing on this paper, describing Dad, the morning of the Garden Club meeting. These walnut-brown stains were remnants of Mickey Foust's life. How could I have missed seeing them when I gathered everything off the table, when the smears would have been brilliant red?

Well, everything was brilliant red then,

is the likeliest explanation. Blood was everywhere. I shouldn't be surprised to find it here now.

I set the dregs of my ice cream cone in the sink and methodically leafed through the rest of the binder. Except for a few pages at the beginning, where the blood-ied page had soaked through, the binder was unharmed.

I would copy my work, the three and a fraction paragraphs of character descrip-tion, onto a clean sheet and trash this one. I sat down to do it, anxious to be rid of the ugly reminder of Mickey's ugly death.

Before I'd copied five words, I saw what Mickey had left me.

14

Of course, I must be imagining things. Mickey couldn't have done this with two bullet holes in his head. Besides, even if he hadn't died instantly, the unfortunate boy was lying on the floor, the notebook out of reach on the table.

And yet, plain as plain, here was a circle on the page, as if a finger dipped in blood had drawn it, around the word 'father.'

Perhaps the murderer had done it. Serial killers sometimes leave messages, subconsciously wanting to be caught. I read that in a ladies' magazine. Did three murders qualify Preble City's killer for serial status? Is there protocol for that sort of thing?

I must show this bloody page to Paul.

I'd rather go to the dentist.

Experienced at procrastinating a dental appointment to the limit, I could certainly procrastinate about contacting Paul. He was busy, after all. The last thing I wanted was to pester him the way I'd been pestering Jerry Joe.

I tore a clean (literally) sheet of paper from the notebook and began to think in ink.

Mickey raps, gets no response, and walks big as you please into the kitchen. He's seen the commotion next door and figures he has some time to snoop. It's money and a hot meal he's after. The old patsy might even put him up in her guest room for a day or a week.

First, he checks the refrigerator, sighing an expletive at its bleak shelves. He peeks into cupboards, finds a box of cookies, takes them out of their wrapper by the handful and pops them like peanuts as he roams deeper into the house. He tours from room to room, opening closet doors, pulling out drawers to stir and slam.

The summer storm blows closer, rolling thunder at the town. Mickey yanks out the nightstand drawer and whistles as he lifts out my Smith and Wesson. He jabs it carelessly into the back waistband of his jeans.

Now he returns to the kitchen, pours himself a glass of milk, sits at the table. Idly drawing the YOW notebook to him, he flips through it, reading bits and pieces, snorting at the fancies of an elderly mind.

A shadow blots the screen door.

Mickey squints at the figure who opens the door and slips inside. To show he isn't worried, he jams his hand into the cookie bag for another helping.

'You're the kid who was at the Linebarger place when Lisa Norvell was killed,' the newcomer — Rosie Hoffsteder, if we're to believe her suicide note — murmurs.

'Depends,' Mickey says, taking a hearty swig of milk. 'What's on your mind?'

'The question is, what's in yours?'

The androgynous silhouette — still not recognizable as Rosie — brings Lisa's Smith and Wesson out of purse or pocket and straight-arms it forward to point at Mickey's head.

Reflexively, Mickey ducks, but at that range it's useless. Two thunderous shots in rapid succession send Mickey sprawling across the table. His big-knuckled hands, grasping at nothing, scatter the cookies and sluice the milk to the floor. His bloody face thuds down between his outstretched arms.

The killer steps closer to look at his/her handiwork and sees my pistol behind Mickey's slumped back. Tossing the murder weapon to the floor with his/her gloved hand, the killer slides the gun from Mickey's waistband and secretes it about his or her person before checking the street, slithering outside, and returning to business as usual.

Mickey stirs. He drags his left hand, the one beside his good eye, in exquisitely slow motion to the blue notebook, knocks aside the cover, and tries to focus on a word that he read earlier. His finger crawls through a convenient pool of blood, and then it creeps around the six letters — 'father' — barely making the circuit before helplessly sliding from the page.

Senseless, Mickey cants sideways in the chair until he overbalances and falls, oblivious to the lump of gun under his shoulder, never to know how it all turns out.

That's one of the reasons I'll resist

death to the death. There's always something going on that I want to see through to its conclusion. Who'll win the presidential election? What will the new library look like? Will the Reds win the league? Stay tuned.

Right along with that is my determination to die only in winter, so as not to miss any nice days.

Rather proud of my murder scenario, I next turned my attention to why Mickey chose 'father' to highlight. If he had enough strength left to do that, why didn't he print the killer's name instead?

He didn't know the killer by name.

I was beginning to wish I'd gone into police work instead of teaching. One shouldn't consider it fun, but it was certainly exhilarating.

Mickey couldn't write his assailant's name because he didn't know it, but he connected this person with a father in some way.

I doubted that a priest was our man — definitely not Father Cameron, who was as stout as a walrus and almost as mobile. That left a biological father for the killer. I picked up my pen again.

It is early evening, and the trees draw long shadows across the grounds of the Linebarger place. A red Jeep chugs to a stop in the driveway and two people alight, a petite blonde woman and a man whose face is as sunless as a pit. They stroll toward the house, not touching one another, though they have touched abundantly in the past.

Inside the close, musty-smelling mansion, Mickey Foust wakens from a Technicolor dream of food and women. Scrubbing at his hair with both hands, he freezes, hearing voices. An owner, here to evict him from this squatter's paradise of silent, empty rooms?

Peering between the boards that bar the windows of his second-story camp site, he sees the foreshortened figures of a woman and man as they disappear beneath the front porch roof. He can hear them moving south around the house, and he follows them from window to window, listening to their arguing.

'Don't think you can threaten me,' the female voice rises. 'I bought myself a gun.

Isn't that a hoot? The man who was so great in bed? Father of my baby? And now I've got to have a gun to feel safe around him.'

'Put that away, Lisa. Don't be such a damned idiot.'

'What is this place, anyway? I wanted somewhere private to talk, not a god-damned mausoleum.'

'You wanted to talk? Talk.'

Mickey slips around to the next window, tracking their progress into the side yard. By squeezing close to the grimy glass, he can sight straight down past the plywood barrier and watch the woman bend to pick a yellow flower from a bed beside the cellar door.

'Ten thousand dollars. That's my price for keeping my mouth shut about Heidi.'

'You think I'm made of money? I haven't got that kind of money.'

'Honey, we're just talking down payment here. Next year, I'll want more, and every year till that little girl starts to drive and drink and create scandals of her own. You want respectability? You want Heidi? You buy it right here from Ms. Lisa

297

Norvell. Otherwise, I'm screaming 'father' so loud — '

The man lunges; the gun glints high between their struggling bodies. Mickey throws himself away from the window, anticipating the shot, which crashes like an ax on hard wood. The second shot never comes, and Mickey gradually relaxes. By the time he sidles to the window for another look, the man is closing the cellar door, dusting his hands. The man peers around the yard as he crams the pistol into his waistband and flaps his shirt tail loose to cover it. Sensing that the man is about to tip his face to scan the house, Mickey backs away, picking up a convenient two-by-four and holding it like a bunter's bat.

After five minutes of intense listening, when all he hears are birds scrambling on the roof and a small plane engine fading in and out on the breeze, Mickey approaches the window and peers down. No one is there.

Still carrying the board, he returns to the front bedroom window. The red Jeep sits deserted, beckoning him to come *search it for valuables. For a time, he watches and waits, still wary. He stands staring at nothing, formulating a way to make some big money for once in his life.*

He will lie low and watch the newspapers; eventually he'll figure out who this man is, and the man will be so thankful that Mickey has kept his secret, the man will gladly give Mickey a thousand bucks. Maybe even two.

Mickey slides down to sit cross-legged on the gritty floorboards, digging in his shirt pocket for I-don't-know-what-kind of drugs to fly his already half-baked brain.

I laid aside my pen and shook the tension out of my fingers. A neighbor's lawn mower hit something alien, squealed, and died. It reminded me that I should telephone the Scalper boy to do my lawn again. His name is Scalpetty, but Scalper better describes what he does to the grass and how much he charges for the privilege.

Who was Heidi's father? How could I find out? Turning all my evidence and conclusions over to Paul would be an immense relief — like sliding into a hot bath after a day of stripping old paint. But I couldn't.

I couldn't because the centerpiece of my information, the blood-highlighted word 'father', resided in the middle of my secret garden, my YOW materials. To show Paul would be to expose my foolish old-lady notion that I could be an author.

This epiphany hit me so hard, my eyes watered. Of course. This was the reason I had not yet taken my squalid typewriter to the repair shop. This was why I had failed to write the first word to send to Mr. Golden. As long as I didn't send him anything, I could continue to pretend that I was a writer, that my $395 would make me a publishable author.

But if I submitted the eagerly awaited assignment, Mr. Golden would have to criticize it. Worse, he might be honest and lie about my chances, coaxing me ever nearer the brink of rejection as I paid my five easy instalments.

Three hundred ninety-five dollars! I could have bought a bread-making machine and a year's supply of flour for that.

Stretching across the table to whip a paper napkin from its fallacious rolling-pin holder, I dabbed my hot eyes and nose.

On Monday, I would phone the city and find out where to get birth records.

★ ★ ★

Sunday arrived first, however. I slept late again, having failed to sleep properly at the allotted time. Once I was on my feet and moving, breakfast didn't sing its usual siren song. Instead, although I didn't deserve it, I made myself a fine lunch of medium-rare broiled steak, a baked potato, and broccoflower in a bacon and cream sauce. Preparing and eating it didn't take enough precious time. Soon the rest of the day stretched before me, nearly ten hours of sunlight and gloomy thoughts.

One of the gloomiest was my acknowledgment that I cared what people thought. I'd believed myself old enough to be beyond worrying about my reputation. After all, hadn't I been willing to break the law — and a window — to gain experience for my writing?

Yet here I was, furtively stowing the Your Own Write text and notebook in the bottom of the bottom drawer of my bedroom dresser, under my winter underwear, having reread my copy of the agreement to confirm that not only could I not have a refund, I must pay the full tuition to the bitter end.

I would have vented my frustration in a scathing expose, if I had known how to write.

As I kicked the drawer shut, I heard it. A motorcycle coming up the street. I wanted to be alone to brood, and not have to smile and be pleasant to anyone, least of all Julian, who might be on the verge of being a pest — checking up on me every other day.

But the sound worsened. It doubled, tripled, became an army of snarling engines. I hurried to the living-room windows. The shaded, normally sleepy street writhed with men on motorcycles. I stepped back, hand to throat, hoping all the neighbors had gone out of town for the weekend. Julian's bulk separated itself from the crowd, and he strode up the driveway.

I met him at the kitchen screen door and he greeted me, pleased as pudding. 'I brought Lisa's friends for you to meet. They want to offer their help, too, what with you trying to find Lisa's killer and all.'

'Dear, dear. I'm afraid the house is in no condition to receive guests — '

'We don't want to come in. We'll just congregate in your backyard.'

'I don't have enough chairs or any refreshments — '

'We brought our own.' He swung what looked like a six-pack of beer up for me to see. 'We can sit on the grass. You weren't going anywhere, were you? We won't stay long.' He leaned closer to the screen to confide, 'These guys aren't Angels either.' I had the distinct impression this was supposed to be reassuring.

And so a few minutes later, I found myself seated on a faded green canvas director's chair brought from my garage, surrounded by as surreal a group of people as I had ever encountered close up. Six burly men, counting Julian, and two scrawny young women lounged about on the ground, popping tabs and unscrewing caps from assorted drinks. A babble of unfamiliar words reinforced my sense of the absurdity of the situation: 'air shifter kit . . . lightweight fairing . . . stators, rotors, armatures . . . brake bleeding . . . chick magnet . . . There were surprisingly few curse words from such a ferocious-looking crew. Or perhaps I just didn't recognize them amidst the new jargon.

Here, indeed, were characters aplenty to inspire fiction, if I were a writer.

Julian introduced them all. Eric had a yellow-toothed grin and shaggy white-blond hair. Rod's muscled arms rippled with tattoos, and the gold hoop in his left ear matched the one in his nostril. George's eyes glared wildly two different directions. Red-haired Dave displayed a split lip, two broken teeth, and a cut on one cheek, neatly stitched with black thread.

'This is Jugger.' Julian waved to the last male, whose black leather vest didn't begin to meet across his hairy sunburned chest.

'What kind of parent would name a child Jugger?' I hoped I joked.

He frowned and I instantly regretted my levity. 'It's short for juggernaut. That's . . . ' He tilted back his head to stare at the treetops, apparently the better to recall. 'That's a noun. It means a massive, inexorable force or object that crushes whatever is in its path.'

I was genuinely dazzled.

His face relaxed into a sweet smile — angelic, if Julian would allow the term. 'My real name is Kevin.' The smile segued into a frown again. 'What kind of parent would name a kid Tirzzy?'

'My real name is Tirzah Quince Quizenberry.'

'Oh.' He looked blank.

But it was the girls who broke my heart. Casey and Britt. Wearing white undershirts, black leather pants and jackets, army boots, and black nailpolish. Casey's hair stood out in tortured pink spikes. Britt's hung in multiple pigtails tied with neon shoelaces. Between them, they'd endured at least a dozen ear piercings, plus one navel and one tongue.

I found it hard to look at them as we talked, my eyes shying away from the bored worldliness in theirs.

The backyard was pleasantly warm, with a kiss of breeze. Bees and butterflies swooped around my flower borders. I stopped worrying about the neighbors being scandalized.

Julian pushed up from his sprawl on the grass and stood, clapping his hands for attention. 'Mrs. Quizenberry has a question or two for us.' He stepped aside to give me the floor — the ground — and I woke a little panicky from my daydream of nothing.

'You know,' Julian coached. 'Lisa. Jay-Jay.'

'Right. Yes. Do any of you happen to know a man who Lisa called Jay-Jay?'

General rumblings of perplexed negation.

'He looks like Dick or Jerry Van Dyke,' I added.

No one seemed any more enlightened.

'All right then, how about this? Did Lisa give any of you anything to safekeep for her? Anything she might have written? Like a diary or a letter to be opened in the event of her death?'

They all thought about it. I could see each one wanted to be the hero who possessed the missing information. But no one could, because no one did.

'Never mind. Thank you,' I said. 'It was only an idea.'

'Lisa was real private,' Jugger growled. 'She didn't talk about herself. You know?'

Britt's hairdo bobbed with her nodding. 'Real, you know, private,' she confirmed.

After a decent interval, the assembly arose as one, deposited their empty bottles and cans in my trash barrel, and headed toward the street. Julian lingered to thank me and remind me to call if I needed anything at all. Engines wakened, throttles bellowed, and the parade rode off. I waved, but none of them saw me. It would have been fun, after all, to hear what my neighbors thought — and my trashman, when he saw all those bottles and cans.

Although the afternoon had produced no clues to Lisa's death, I was glad to eliminate her friends as suspects. They might not be angels, but they certainly didn't seem like devils, either.

★ ★ ★

On my way to the city building Monday morning, I stopped at the police station to see how Paul was progressing without benefit of my suppressed evidence.

Managing to look him in the eye, I asked one of the questions uppermost in my mind. 'Did you find cookies and milk at the scene of Mickey's murder?'

Paul was not alone in his office. A uniformed young man with a Valentino hairdo forced himself up from the visitors' chair when I arrived. Now he eyed me as if memorizing me for future testimony in court.

'Cookies and milk?' Paul smiled.

'Never mind, I don't want to know. What I do want to know is, did Mickey die as soon as he was shot?'

Paul's smile wavered. 'We can't calculate that precisely. Death was either instantaneous or moments later. Why do you ask?'

'Would he have been able to do anything?'

'Do anything?'

'Could he think? Be conscious? With

308

two bullets through his ruined head?'

Paul's colleague spoke up. 'I've seen a guy on steroids take a shot square between the eyes and keep on coming at the shooter. It's like cutting a chicken's head off and the body thrashes around on automatic pilot for a while.'

'Oh, my. It's just that — the bullets were so big.'

Hiking up his pants, the officer warmed to his topic. 'It doesn't matter what caliber bullet you've got. A 9mm will wipe out a lot of tissue, but a little twenty-two can do worse damage because it ricochets around inside the skull instead of exiting clean.'

'Tirzzy.' Paul's frown had slipped into his voice. 'Why are you asking this?'

'I just wanted to settle it in my mind. Whether he had time to say a prayer or not.' I hoped that I had never mentioned to Paul that I was about as interested in religion as I was in tag-team wrestling.

'Don't you worry, ma'am,' the young policeman said. 'A victim naturally thinks a quick prayer. It's probably as automatic as his sphincters letting loose.'

I appreciated the intent of the reassurance

even though it brought forth information I'd have preferred not to stumble into.

'This is Officer Skelly,' Paul said, finally remembering his manners. 'Care to sit down, Tirzzy?'

Shaking my head, I made a half-hearted move toward the door. 'I have things to do, and I'm sure you gentlemen do also. Have you learned anything new about Rosie's death? Did she really swallow all those heartworm pills?'

Paul stroked his tie to lie straight inside his jacket. 'Where did you get the idea it was heartworm pills?'

'It wasn't?'

'She injected herself with euthanasia solution, the stuff her dad uses to put down animals. Death is instantaneous if it hits a vein — at least with dogs and cats, I'm told.'

'Wait a minute.' I parked my fist on my waist. 'I was willing to believe Rosie killed herself by ingesting too many pills — how would a murderer force her to do that? But an injection — he could easily jab her, take her completely by surprise.'

'It wasn't murder, Tirzzy. Remember,

there was a suicide note. Rosie's finger-prints were on it and on the syringe.' Young Skelly swung his attentive face from Paul to me as if we were a tennis match. I did not intend to miss my point.

'Paul, the murderer pressed her fingers to those items after she was dead.'

'Tirzzy, there is no murderer except for Rosie.'

'What if I could show you that someone besides Rosie killed Mickey Foust? Then would you entertain the notion that she didn't kill herself either?'

'What do you mean show me? You've got some kind of proof?'

'Not yet.' It galled me to back down, but it would have galled me worse to confess to withholding evidence.

Paul yanked a wrapped cigar from his breast pocket to point at me. 'Not yet and not ever. I'm not asking you, I'm telling you. Stop meddling in what's police business.'

Officer Skelly swung around to see if I could handle a spike that wicked.

'It's out,' I told him, retiring from the court by way of the office door.

311

City Offices Will Be Closed Tomorrow, Tuesday. The black-markered cardboard sign was masking-taped to the glass door of the city building. I pushed through and approached the reception counter, where an elderly man I didn't know was trying to convince the receptionist that his neighbor was pirating cable TV.

I also didn't know the receptionist, but apparently the man did, for he kept addressing her as Honey. 'Honey, I know you think I'm crazy, but it's God's truth. See, Brady has this satellite dish disguised as a trampoline, and I know for a fact he's never paid a dime to the city to use it.'

The old coot looked the way James Dean, bless him, would have looked at eighty — shriveled thin, bald-and-so-what, all the lines of his face sagging his mouth into a perpetual scowl. The young lady who faced off with him had white-blonde hair in a strange cut that reminded me of an A- bomb explosion.

'Sir, you want the cable company. They're a block south. The city has nothing to do with — '

'Is there a reward for turning pirates in?'

'I can't tell you that. You'll have to ask the cable company.'

The girl had more patience than I. Easing up close behind him, I faked a few preliminary coughs, intending to drive him off with an all-out fit, if necessary.

It wasn't necessary. Turning and glaring at me, the man said, 'I wouldn't mind so much Brady stealing the television waves, but his daughters jumping on the dish is about to drive me bonkers.'

'Why are you closed tomorrow?' I asked the young woman, getting my foot in the door although the man had not yet relinquished his place.

Her polite smile shifted into an expression of regret. 'Because of the funeral in the morning. You know. The mayor's sister.'

'It's that soon? They aren't wasting any time, autopsy and all.'

She didn't take up my gauntlet of gossip. 'May I help you?'

The old man swayed and stepped aside, though he didn't move toward the street door. Instead, he stood and watched us go about my business.

'How do I look up a birth notice?' I asked.

'You mean get a copy of a birth certificate?'

'I guess.'

'Recent or historical?'

'Three years old.'

She smiled over my shoulder at someone walking by. 'That's going to be in the county courthouse. The health department.'

'You're in the wrong place,' the old man spoke up. 'The county seat is up at Eaton.'

'Thank you,' I said. 'The cable company is a block south of here.'

I fully intended to drive to Eaton that afternoon, but I made the mistake of telephoning Scott Scalpetty first, and the only day he could mow the lawn this week was today.

While his lanky body plodded behind the shrieking mower, I baked a double batch of molasses cookies — Velma's favorite — and decided what to wear to Rosie's funeral.

I waited until I heard the newspaper

slap Velma's porch floor, and then I carried over the dish of cookies swathed in Saran wrap. Knocking at the screen door, I hummed hopefully, until I realized the tune was *How Much Is That Doggie in the Window?*

15

Velma's slow tread announced her approach. She pushed the door open and said, 'Well?'

I shoved the cookies at her. 'Could I check your paper for the time of Rosie's funeral?'

'Come in.'

'It smells like you've been baking too,' I said, following her toward the kitchen.

'That's hot chocolate that boiled over on a burner.'

'Oh.'

'You put on some show yesterday afternoon.'

'Those were friends of Lisa Norvell's. They traveled up from Cincinnati to thank me for my continued efforts to find her murderer. I thought about asking you over. Would you have come?'

'No.'

'I have to go to Eaton tomorrow afternoon or the next day. You want to ride along?'

'Oh, I don't know.'

She walked to the kitchen table. The blue and white checked oilcloth was awash in grocery coupons Velma had been cutting out with a pair of manicure scissors. I used to save coupons, but I was too good at it. I saved them till they expired and threw them away. Velma, on the other hand, redeems her coupons whether she needs the item or not. She was probably still stocking up on dog food rather than letting one-dollar-off go to waste.

'Come on, Velma. A little trip away from home would do you good.'

'What do you want to go to Eaton for?' She lifted the evening paper out of the coupon debris and held it out to me.

'Well . . . ' I spread open the *Inkling* and pretended to be sidetracked by it.

'I thought so. More Hoffsteder nonsense.' Folding her arms, Velma waited for me to deny it.

'Glinda Graves is getting married again,' I said, genuinely sidetracked now. 'What does this make — five?'

'So many men, so little time.'

'What's she got that we haven't got?'

'Legs that look like she's wearing hip boots.'

I laughed louder than it was worth, because it was such a relief to laugh at all.

'I'm not in the notion to go anywhere tomorrow,' Velma said. She sat down at the table and picked up the puny scissors to pinch loose another flyer coupon.

'How about Wednesday, then?' I hated to beg, but I wasn't too proud to do it.

'I don't want to promise.'

'No promises,' I agreed. 'If you can't go Wednesday, I'll go by myself. The fact is, I could probably just make a phonecall and not drive over there at all, but I thought the trip might be pleasant. Stop at a mall. Have a nice lunch.'

'I'll let you know.'

'Here it is. Hoffsteder. Ten-thirty Tuesday at Foley's Funeral Home. I thought I ought to go to the service. I don't really want to.'

'I doubt if I'll want to go anywhere Wednesday either,' Velma said.

Her scissors needed oiling. They wheezed through the paper, perpetually trying to turn corners with their blades. I knew Velma had a better tool for the job somewhere. She was just being stubborn.

'Glory, what's that?' she said.

Now that she mentioned it, I could hear it, too. Not motorcycles this time, but almost as loud. I held aside Velma's crisp pink curtains to confirm that a long white bus was hiss-squealing to a full stop across the mouth of my driveway.

'Tirzzy, you do beat all,' Velma said, watching with me as Julian, resplendent in a navy and gold chauffeur's uniform, hopped down to the curb.

Sweeping off the billed and braided cap, he smoothed at his already smooth head and strutted toward my house. I could see faces at all the windows of the bus, tourists with avid interest in their strange surroundings.

'Hide me under your bed,' I said to Velma.

'Certainly not. Go out there and see what he wants. I swear, living next to you is more entertaining than having cable TV.'

Denied sanctuary, I went home, dragging my feet even more than usual. Out of the corner of my eye, I could see waving from the bus windows. I hailed Julian before my door splintered under his knocking.

'Miz Tirzzy,' he sang out. 'I've here to see if you'd like to go to Graceland with us. Had a cancellation. Broken hip, poor soul. So we got room for one more, and we'll give you half an hour to pack. You can pay the fifty bucks dues whenever you got it.'

'It's sweet of you to think of me, but I really don't — '

'It'd be ideal. We're going to be gone ten days, so I won't be around here to keep an eye on you. Go with us, you'll be safe as fleas on a junkyard dog.'

While he had his back turned, his charges were escaping off the bus. Two white-haired ladies went across the street to inspect the Kellermans' irises. A pair of unsteady gentlemen circled around testing the bus tires with the tips of their canes. An overweight woman lowered herself to the curb and stripped off her shoes and socks, then waded into my freshly cut lawn with evident delight.

'What do you say, Mrs. Quizenberry?'

From the end of the driveway, a tiny woman with the painful-looking gait of a hurrying monkey called ahead of herself, 'I want to use the bathroom.'

'This isn't a rest stop, Peggy. You can use the facilities on the bus.'

She immediately and cheerfully changed course.

'No, Julian,' I said. 'I can't come with you. I can't leave right now. I'm very close to the solution to Lisa's death.'

'No lie! Well, damn, how can I abandon you when it's getting intense?'

I patted his arm. 'The police will protect me. You go on and have a good time.'

'Damn. You sure?'

By now, the entire busload must have been wandering the street, my yard, the neighbors' yards. Several inmates grouped around Julian and me, openly listening to our conversation. I helped him shoo them toward the bus.

He climbed on board and honked the air horn twice, calling his faithful. They straggled back, nodding and speaking to me as they climbed the steps. After a head count, followed by a roundup of three strays in Velma's back yard, Julian raised his hand in farewell and swished the folding doors shut. I stepped back and waved at all the gyrating hands as the bus fired up. In a moment, it had bulldozed down the narrow street and out of sight.

I stood a while, relishing the silence.

★ ★ ★

Tuesday morning, Dewey Foley's son Bryon helped me up the steps to the funeral home double doors. His black hair and black suit gleamed in the sunlight, and he smelled like too much cologne.

The white three-story house was once a fine Victorian home full of life instead of death. Stepping into it now felt like diving under water, dark and sibilant with low voices. Even the organ sounded like the municipal pool's, except it wasn't playing *Cruising Down the River*.

Bryon delivered me to the remembrance book on its walnut pedestal, and I signed in. Two-thirds of the pages were filled with names, presumably from last night's visitation, for there weren't that many people in evidence at the moment. Handing the pen to the next person to arrive — Jerry Joe's too-thin secretary in a becoming dress the color of coral bells — I moved on into the main room.

It is always good to have plenty of flowers where a body lies in state, to give the mourners something else to look at and discuss. On the far wall, Rosie's casket was almost submerged in masses and banks and swarms of blooms, their colors as jumbled as their scents. I caught a glimpse of her pale face floating in the sea before Bonita Hoffsteder stepped in the way to adjust something in the coffin.

A dozen visitors toured the floral display, bending to read the cards and play name-that-flower. Another dozen stood beside or sat upon the bronze folding chairs which fanned out in rows from the casket as if Rosie would be performing some entertainment. Front and center, Dr. and Mrs. Hoffsteder waited for the curtain, he sitting on the edge of his chair, elbows on knees and hands clasped, she sitting sideways with her back to him, talking to a knot of friends.

I see-sawed from one foot to the other, dreading the requisite parade past the deceased and the impotent condolences to the family. Thumping myself down in a back-row seat, I fanned myself with the program Bryon must have given me.

John Junior joined Bonita, and they stood with their backs to Rosie to confer with the ever-inanimated Reverend Eby. John's suit and haircut must have been new. He kept shrugging the one and palming down the other. Several times, he grasped Bonita's arm and urged her into the conversational group, as if she had a tendency to creep into reverse.

Jerry Joe and his fiancée hustled in and sat down next to his father, leaning across him to speak to Cynthia. May Ruth had gained a few pounds since I saw her last, some of them in her long hair, an artful tangle so immobilized by hair spray it looked as if a careless jostle would shatter it. She put an arm around Jerry Joe's shoulders, and her diamond engagement ring flashed.

'Hello, Tirzzy,' Sylvia Butterbaugh said, coming from behind to pause beside my chair. Loreen was with her, both of them wearing navy dresses and white accessories, like me. A sort of senior citizen dress uniform.

'Are things back to normal at your house?' Sylvia leaned in to ask, and the ghost of cigarettes past brushed between us.

'I'm fine. Did you just arrive?'

They nodded. Loreen squinted at the wall of flowers. 'Have you found the Garden Club arrangement? Ordinarily, we wouldn't have spent the money on someone who hadn't paid her dues yet, but under these circumstances . . . ' She pinched her lips together and shook her head, marveling at these circumstances.

'I haven't done anything except come in and sit down. I was trying to work up the courage to speak to Cynthia. Maybe you'll let me tag along with you.'

Sylvia led the way, and Loreen lagged next, admiring flowers and speaking to everyone, and I brought up the rear, feeling like one of the Andrews Sisters on our way to sing for the troops. We regrouped beside the casket, which was open to Rosie's waist, giving the impression that she was lying under a Dutch door. A quartet of peach and green cymbidium orchids clung to the bosom of her white silk dress.

I hoped she had enjoyed such a corsage at least once while she was living.

Sighing, I turned to pay my respects to Cynthia. She looked up and through me, offering her limp hand to be pressed rather than shaken. Beside her, Dr. Hoffsteder nodded, his eyes as welcoming as patches of black glare ice.

'There aren't adequate words for times like this,' I said, letting go of Cynthia's moist hand and fighting the impulse to rub my palm on my skirt. 'I'm sorry for your loss.'

She didn't answer. Her dazed expression might have indicated shock or drugs, except that Cynthia usually looked this way. I stepped aside to let Loreen say her piece.

This put me in front of May Ruth, who flashed her dimples at me in recognition.

'Mrs. Quizenberry. How are you? I haven't talked to you in a coon's age.'

That was true, assuming that the coon wasn't living at the time I invented the telephone-contest lie to obtain Jerry Joe's unlisted number.

Jerry Joe made a half-hearted movement to stand, and subsided when I told him to sit still. Meaning to move on in a minute, I felt myself warming to May Ruth as she chattered about the good old days of diagramming sentences and conjugating verbs. She had never done either wisely or too well, but she'd always managed to be cheerful about the assignment.

Jerry Joe sat perfectly relaxed, one leg bent across the opposite knee, a hint of a smile on his lips, watching his bride-to-be. Whenever I dropped a 'yes' or 'no' into the dialogue, he'd snap his eyes up, quick as a thrown switch, to study my face.

Loreen crowded me over to make room for Sylvia in front of Cynthia, and May Ruth exclaimed, 'Mrs. Previn. I haven't seen you in a coon's age.'

I circled around through a vacant row

of seats and came up on the other side of Cynthia, where John Junior had Bonita pinned between him and a delegation of tellers from the First National Bank. The tellers eased on toward the casket, and I stepped into the vacancy.

'Did you find yourself some eggs, Mrs. Quizenberry?' John asked, reminding me that he saw through my subterfuge, but smiling as he said it, no hard feelings.

'Not as fresh as yours would have been. I'm truly sorry about your sister.'

'She had a short, unhappy life.' He half-twisted around to gaze at Rosie. 'Maybe this is best for her and everyone concerned.'

'Maybe.' The concerned one for whom it was definitely the best was whoever had killed her. I couldn't help glancing around the congregation, looking for guilt written all over a face.

The incessant, canned organ music stopped in mid-chord, leaving the room to rustlings and low voices. Dewey Foley, arms spread like a shepherding angel, was urging people toward seats. Reverend Eby had taken his station at the lectern, peering over his bifocals at the settling audience. Sylvia caught my eye and pointed at a row halfway back, and I nodded. I intended to make some closure statement to John and Bonita, but they had already turned away to converse with someone else.

Arriving at the chair Sylvia had picked for me, I found Grandma Becker hunkered in the next one over. Grandma has been Grandma seemingly forever, though at one time she must have been known by her given name of Mildred. She's one of those women whom it is impossible to picture as ever being young. Face as wrinkled as a hedge apple, eyes veiled with cataracts, voice like coal dribbling down a chute, she welcomed me to my chair by patting it.

'Four hundred and two,' she gurgled.

Knowing her hobby, I was not stumped by this greeting. 'My, my. You've been to as many funerals as Dewey.'

'More.' She waved her opera glasses languidly and dropped that hand back into her black rayon lap.

Sylvia nudged me from the other side and nodded at the front. 'Who's that?'

'John Junior's son and granddaughter,' I whispered.

Darrell stood a moment talking to his parents, Heidi on his hip, her golden legs looking thin and long below the pink ruffled dress hiked up to her white ruffled panties. Then Darrell sat down with her on his lap, giving me a good view of her blonde hair skimmed back in a French braid fastened with purple plastic butter-flies.

I put my hand against my heart, finally feeling a wash of grief. Not for Rosie, though she deserved more sympathy than she was getting. My pain was for poor little innocent Heidi, who had nothing and everything to do with the woes of her family.

Reverend Eby cleared his throat and asked us to pray. I always bow my head in respect for the believers in the company, but I don't shut my eyes and I don't say amen. Still thinking about Heidi, I was slow to raise my face at the end of the prayer, and Grandma jabbed me with a sharp finger as if I'd dozed off and begun to snore.

The preacher read us his generic funeral message in a voice as scintillating as warm tar. While he carefully avoided any mention of shortcomings in Rosie's character, such as tendencies to commit suicide or murder, I stared at the back of Heidi's head. The vulnerable stalk of neck. The tiny ears. She turned her face to whisper to Darrell, and a gleam of gold indicated she'd undergone an ear piercing. Why adults want to inflict their notions of beauty and fashion on a baby who can't vote has always been beyond me.

As she continued to confide in Darrell, I narrowed my eyes, trying to make out something odd about her ear. The earring wasn't on the lobe, but higher, on the narrower edge of the opening. Perhaps my sight deceived, but Heidi didn't seem to have an earlobe. Had it been lost in an accident? In *the* accident? I waited for her to turn her head the other way and show the opposite ear. With nothing else to occupy me, I noticed that there was something unusual about Darrell's ears as well.

'Let me borrow your binoculars,' I murmured to Grandma, who struggled to oblige without choking herself in the leather strap around her neck.

By the time I had the focus right, Heidi and Darrell were facing one another in solemn consultation, one small ear and one large ear bare to my confirmation. Why did John Junior spin me that tale about Heidi's miraculous arrival in a pumpkin seat under a corn stalk? Anyone could see she had her father Darrell's ears.

Grandma tugged at the dangling strap of her opera glasses. Ignoring her, I twitched them left to pick up the back of John's head. Even from that bad angle, I could tell his ears had a normal amount of flap hanging below. Bonita wore quarter-sized white earrings that would have been impossible without lobes. Cynthia's bouffant hair hid her ears. Dr. Hoffsteder —

Grandma's grip on the glasses strap began to drag my head toward my knees. Still, I had a few seconds' perfect view of John Senior's surprisingly truncated ears before Grandma won the tug of war. Muttering, she reclaimed her property while I wondered why I had never noticed the vet's peculiar ears. Probably it was because I had always been too busy noticing his peculiar eyes.

Did Jerry Joe have his father's ears? I couldn't see that far, and I knew better than to ask Grandma for another turn. It didn't matter anyway. Obviously earlobe deficiency was a recessive gene in the Hoffsteder family.

Obviously, Heidi was a Hoffsteder.

My head ached from too much thinking and the oversweet floral perfumes cloying the room. Mercifully, Reverend Eby ran down, and the invisible organ began to pump the room full of *In the Garden*. Everyone stood and soldiered toward the exit.

'I've heard better eulogies,' Grandma addressed my back. 'Can I ride with you to the cemetery?

It wasn't my intention to attend the graveside service, but I owed Grandma a favor, and I remained curious about the configuration of Jerry Joe's ears. The mourners clotted along the shady street discussing sports and recipes — life does go on — while Dewey and the pallbearers brought Rosie out the side portico. They slid the casket into the hearse as smoothly as a loaf of bread into the oven.

★ ★ ★

The ground around Rosie's burial site was soggy. May Beth's spike heels kept sinking, and she had to hang on to the back of Cynthia's folding chair to keep from tipping backwards. Then the mud began to swallow the chair's rear legs, till Cynthia's posture was definitely on the recline. Noticing, John Senior urged his wife to her feet and held her hand as the minister finished his scripture reading.

All the while, I observed earlobes — Heidi's, Darrell's, and Dr. Hoffsteder's. No one else in the semi-circle of friends and relatives listened with ears of little lobe. That included Jerry Joe, who prowled the perimeter of the scattered group, hands in pockets, jiggling change.

I felt the same, restless way — longing for the ceremony to be at an end. The only pleasant part about it was the sight of Heidi's sleeping face against Darrell's sturdy shoulder. The twinkling earring lulled me like a mesmerist's swaying charm, and I scarcely heard the final prayer.

'Come on. I got to take a nap,' Grandma said, tugging me toward the Buick by a pinch of my sleeve. 'The Smith interment is this afternoon.'

'What Smith is that?'

'The one that died.' She laughed like air leaking out of a tire.

Helping Grandma into the car, I gazed across the roof at what was left of Rosie's funeral party. All the Hoffsteders huddled on the central path, no doubt discussing who would ride home with whom. Heidi ran around and around them, her pink dress a whirling peony, with white and yellow carnations clutched in both hands.

I had to bite my tongue to keep from shouting at her to throw them down.

* * *

I'm not a nap person. Like Thomas Edison, I consider sleep a necessary waste of time.

I lay down on the couch after my cold cuts and fruit cocktail lunch, not to sleep but to reason. It was annoying to rouse up two hours later to the realization I'd been dreaming instead of thinking. To add to my disgust, I couldn't even think what I had been dreaming.

When I'd used the bathroom, I slouched to the kitchen and poured myself some iced tea. Standing at the screen door to sip it, I tried to decide whether Velma was at home. I wanted to remind her of the trip to Eaton tomorrow, so that she could enjoy the satisfaction of refusing my invitation.

Her garage door was shut, her house windows were open, nothing moved except the starlings and robins beating the grass for worms. I'd no sooner decided to walk over and see if she was there, than here she came out of her house with her black patent purse under her arm. She disappeared into the garage, and after a minute the big door swooped open, she drove out, and the door thumped down again.

I don't have an automatic garage door.

During the summer, the Buick sits out, and in the winter, I drive too infrequently to justify the luxury. I'm more tempted to get such a device since Sylvia Butterbaugh found that her electric door had other uses. It exterminated a mouse for her, though how she got the animal to stand under the descending weight was never adequately explained. After that, she used the door to compact pop cans for recycling. The Brazil nut experiment was, I believe, a failure.

Velma disappeared down the street, and the telephone rang. Grateful for something to do, I hurried to answer it.

'Hello,' Paul said. I could hear the pup-pup-pup of a cigar being lit.

'Good afternoon.' I smiled as if he could see me.

'Yes, it is. I just wanted to let you know that the district attorney is closing the files on Lisa Norvell and Mickey Foust. He's satisfied that Rosetta Hoffsteder's suicide note was genuine. You can pack away your magnifying glass and deerstalker.'

I rubbed at my forehead with a thumb

and forefinger, annoyed and disappointed by Paul's tactlessness.

'Shall we celebrate with dinner tomorrow night? It'll be my treat, because I'm a good winner,' he said.

'Not tomorrow. There's someplace I have to go.'

'Thursday, then?'

'Thursday would be fine. Good-bye, Paul.'

By Thursday, I should be able to carry on a lively dinner conversation, beginning with disclosure of the name of Heidi's father, and ending — I would screw my courage to the sticking point — with my producing Mickey's dying message.

I might be an old fool, but I wasn't too foolish to admit it. Heidi's future might depend on my speaking up about her

The afternoon inched by. I wasn't in the mood for TV or for reading. What I felt like doing was the activity I'd forsworn — writing. I resolutely tamped down the fledgling lines of a poem that grew, unbidden, in my mind. I wished for an out-of-town friend to whom I could write an overlong letter that would siphon off the verbal swamp that was making my head swim.

I resorted to solitaire on the kitchen table. Letting the luck of the draw dictate my every action, not having to reason or defend my choices, I found peace. Slip, slip, slip, slap — over and over, card on card, suit on suit, while my life ticked away.

I'd just dealt a new hand with too many black cards showing when I heard an automobile engine mutter to a stop. I gave Velma a minute to get clear of her seat belt, and then I pushed away from the table and strolled to the screen door.

But Velma had not arrived home. The motor I'd heard belonged to a sporty red something that blocked the Buick in my own driveway. One foot propped possessively on the rear bumper of the little convertible, talking with the Kellermans from across the street, Jerry Joe Hoffsteder appeared very much at ease.

My heart gave a start of unhappy surprise before I reassured myself. No intelligent murderer would come to his prospective victim's house in still broad daylight, park his sports coupé with its

HIZONER license plate in her driveway, and engage her neighbors in conversation before breaking into her house to polish her off.

I inserted the puny door hook into its useless eye and waited for developments. The conversation, too far away for me to catch my words, was interspersed with brief, good-natured laughter.

At length, unable to stand the suspense anymore, I unhooked the door and stepped out on my dappled porch. Shading my eyes, I waited for someone to notice me.

Mona Kellerman obliged by waving, and her husband raised one hand in greeting. Jerry Joe twisted around, dropped his foot off the car, and smiled with all his teeth.

'Hello, Mrs. Q.,' he called jovially. 'I hope you haven't had your supper yet. I've brought Chinese carry-out.' He sorted out a key and sprang the trunk lid open.

The Kellermans withdrew across the street, got into their van, and drove away while Jerry Joe loaded his arms with white cartons, elbowed the trunk shut, and strode at me.

'I'm not hungry,' I said, as if that would stop him in his tracks.

'We don't have to eat right away,' he said, mounting the steps and circling around behind me to juggle open the door. 'I'm full of funeral feast, myself.'

'What do you want, Jerry Joe?' I asked from the porch, letting the door fall shut between us.

Jerry Joe dumped the cartons on my table, scattering the solitaire deck. He bent to retrieve the ace of spades that slithered to the floor.

'I want you to trust me, Mrs. Q.,' he said, pushing wide the screen and crooking his finger at me. 'So we can both get on with our lives. Come on. I'll tell you everything you want to know.'

I'm sure that Eve, if she existed, never coveted any knobby green apple. It was the promise of true stories that caused her to yield to the snake.

I stepped into my kitchen.

16

Jerry Joe made himself at home, opening the refrigerator to stow the Chinese food. He lifted out a can of orange soda and knuckled off the tab.

'You want one too?' He hovered his hand ready to fetch out another of my own pop.

'No. I want you to say your piece and leave. I may have misjudged you, but I don't have to like being with you.'

'Oh-oh. I guess I can't count on your vote in the gubernatorial race.' He lifted the can for several swallows and then used the back of the same hand to wipe his mouth. Looking down, looking around, he said, 'Which of these chairs was Mickey Foust sitting in?'

'That's about enough. You get out or I'm going to phone Paul McMorris.'

'No, wait. I'm sorry. I'm just in a funny — I'm upset today.' He set the pop can on the counter and, hands in pockets, paced that end of the room. 'Rosie's funeral and all. I just want to hit something, you know? I can't settle down. I had to leave the house, my family, get away from all that angst. I'm tired of being on my good behavior, you know? I thought maybe if I made amends with you, things would start turning better again.'

'All right. Let's sit down and you tell me the truth you promised.'

He drew out a chair for me.

'This is my favorite,' I fabricated, picking the one closest at hand and dropping into it, unwilling, yet, to turn my back while he seated me.

'I saw you at the city building yesterday,' he said, taking the chair he'd meant for me. 'I heard you asking about birth records. You're like a pup-dog worrying a sock. You never give it up.'

I considered that a compliment, though I knew it wasn't meant for one. Folding my hands on the table top, I waited for something more interesting to surface.

'And you were staring at Heidi at the funeral. I saw you studying all of us. I could just hear the gears going round in your head.'

An early evening breeze billowed the curtains over the sink. They looked like restless ghosts.

'John said he told you about finding Heidi after Lisa's auto accident,' Jerry Joe went on.

I nodded. 'I'm supposed to believe it was some wild coincidence that Lisa was in his neighborhood and that he found her baby in his field and that the child had earlobes just like Darrell's.'

'Nobody else who heard the story ever questioned it. Course, you can count on the fingers of one hand the number of people who heard the story. No one who could or would make trouble about it till you, that's for sure.'

I reached to take up the deck of cards and shuffle my nervousness away. My theory of Jerry Joe as murderer might be crackpot, but he certainly did have a knack for making me feel threatened.

'You're right, Mrs. Q. Lisa was visiting old John Junior the night of her accident. She had this unwanted infant, see, and John had said that he'd take it.'

My stiff fingers worked the cards

through the cards.

'Thing is, she got there and she changed her mind. She saw the nice place, the farm and the house, the nice well-off family that was eager to take the responsibility and expense of raising her kid, and she went into this dumb female mode, hormones or something, where she just changed her freaking mind. So she loaded the baby back into her Bronco and took off, and she hadn't gone more than half a mile before she lost it, rolled the Bronc, and damn near killed herself.'

'So John knew to search for the baby.'

'Oh, yeah. He found it right away, before the emergency crews arrived. It was like he told you. A miracle landing. Heidi was fine.'

'And he thought Lisa wasn't going to pull through, so why not continue with the unofficial adoption as originally planned.'

'Exactly.'

'How did Lisa know about John in the first place? That he would care for her child?'

'Now, Tirzzy, you know the answer to that one. I told her about him, him about her. Because John's been a sucker for children all his life, and Bonita had female problems that made Darrell an only child. And so I thought of John right away, because I sure didn't want any offspring, not even my own.'

I guess I'd been holding my breath. I breathed out hard now. 'You're right. I knew that. You also didn't want an ex-girlfriend who'd be embarrassing to your political career.'

'Whoa, wait a minute. You sound like you think I killed Lisa.'

'Didn't you?'

He leaned back till the chair teetered on its hind legs, reaching to open a cupboard behind him. 'Got any potato chips to cut the sweet taste of orange soda?'

'No.'

He subsided and the chair thumped back on all fours. 'What was it made you think I murdered Lisa?'

'Fuzzy.'

'I beg your pardon?' His puzzled expression was, I'd have wagered, the first honest face he'd shown since coming onto my property.

'The homeroom hamster. You put flowers in his grip too.'

Jerry Joe threw back his head so that his Adam's apple bulged, and he laughed and laughed. Not knowing whether to be angry or afraid or both, I stood and fixed myself a cup of tea in the microwave, without offering him any. By the time I sat down again, he'd stopped laughing, stopped hiccoughing leftover chuckles, blown his nose, and drunk the last of his pop.

'He bit my finger,' Jerry Joe said, single-handedly crushing the can.

I kept my face a careful blank.

'My sister Rosie killed Lisa. The police said so.'

Sipping my tea, I wished I'd boiled an entire pot full to throw in his face if necessary. It wasn't too late. I stood up again and filled the tea kettle from the tap. The incoming breeze stroked my face like cool feathers. Smacking the kettle onto a burner, I twisted the knob to high.

Leaning against the cabinet, very aware of the splintered bullet holes behind me, I said, 'What happened when Lisa came out of her coma? She remembered Heidi. Did she remember you?'

'Darlin', no woman has ever forgotten me. Can I have some coffee?'

'In a minute.'

'And you know what else sounds good? A homemade dill pickle. Have you got some in your basement?' He grinned up at me expectantly. 'Every old lady has murky jars of pickled cucumbers in her basement.'

I'd diagnosed Jerry Joe as an egomaniac. Maybe he was just maniac. I wished the water would heat faster.

The telephone rang and I jumped as if I'd been scalded. It rang a second time while I waited for Jerry Joe to tell me not to answer it. He didn't, so I did.

'Tirzzy, you hung up so fast earlier today, I forgot to establish what time we should meet at the Heritage — '

'Paul! Jerry Joe Hoffsteder is here,' I rushed to say before Jerry Joe should stop me. He sat smiling, one arm hooked over the back of the chair, perfectly at ease, waiting for his coffee and his pickle.

'Oh? A social call?'

'I'm not sure.'

Jerry Joe idly reached out to draw open the nearest drawer and rooted through it. He found my meat tenderizing hammer, examined it, and dropped it back.

Paul said, 'I'm glad you two are talking at least.'

Jerry Joe brought out my rolling pin. He held it aloft, testing its weight.

'Why don't you come over, Paul? We'll make it a three-way conversation.'

'Sorry, I can't. I've got a crime prevention seminar to give over at the high school in ten minutes.'

I wanted to say that I was trying to prevent a crime myself, but Jerry Joe had set aside the rolling pin to clean his nails with the pull tab from his pop can, and I didn't want to stir him up again.

Some children have a talent for rolling their tongues into a curl, some for wiggling their ears, some for burping on demand. One doesn't usually need such abilities later in life. Still, they're there, dormant and ready. Remembering that the police term for informing is 'belch,' I sent a lusty, gassy exhale along the telephone wires into Paul's ear.

'Sorry,' I said, and did it again.

Jerry Joe shook his head, snorting his amusement.

'Are you all right?' Paul tried to ask while I let loose a third, disgusting burp.

'No,' I said. And then because Jerry Joe glanced up, his eyes glittering and aware, I added, 'Radishes for lunch.'

'Take an antacid. Shall I pick you up at seven Thursday?'

'Fine,' I said, angry with him for being so dense. There was no use blurting out a cry for help. If Jerry Joe was really crazy and/or really meant to kill me, he'd have it accomplished before Paul could locate his car keys.

'How about my making reservations at Hake's Inn for a change,' Paul was saying.

'Fine,' I repeated. I'd never been to Hake's (Farmersville's Finest for Fine Diners) and I doubted I was going to spoil my record.

'Don't order anything with radishes,' Paul said, hanging up.

My kettle of water showed no sign of life, probably due to my having switched on the wrong burner. I scraped the kettle over to the right one.

'So. What do you think, Mrs. Q.?' Jerry Joe said.

'I think . . . ' I took a deep, deep breath, wondering how many I had left. 'I think you and Lisa met and enjoyed a grand affair until she found herself pregnant and you found you loved politics more. I think she didn't have an abortion, even though she didn't want a child, because she thought you'd come around to marrying her if she had your baby. Although . . . ' I sat down to think. 'My impression of Lisa is that she wasn't interested in being committed to one man. She must have loved you very much.'

Jerry Joe shook his head, the knowing smile still stiffening his lips. 'Not me. She loved the idea of being first lady of Ohio.'

'So she gave birth, and she saw that wasn't enough to deter you from your plan to marry May Ruth. Then Lisa asked you to help her find someone to take Heidi so that she could go back to enjoying her independence. She must have thought she might want to reclaim the child someday, or she'd have put her up for legal adoption. She must have felt a smidgen of maternal love.'

I wouldn't judge Lisa for her hedonism. She'd had, after all, poor parental role models.

The kitchen filled with a sudden luminous light as the sun soared out of a nest of clouds. From the living room, Great Grandfather Maynard's clock measured out eight fruity chimes.

I cleared my throat. 'John Junior agreed to take Heidi, and Lisa was delivering her to him the night of the accident. Afterward, when Lisa recovered, she saw how much John and Bonita loved the infant, and how much you loved yourself, and decided to demand money to allow the status to remain quo. She had sense enough — or as it turned out was foolish enough — to buy a gun for her meetings with you.'

Jerry Joe nodded. 'You're doing pretty good. Go on. Just don't forget that Rosie killed her.'

I sipped at my tepid tea. The sun jumped back out of sight, and the room went dim as a church.

'I'm supposed to think that Rosie sacrificed herself to protect the happiness of her two brothers?'

'Why not?'

'Rosie the Razor? I find that unlikely. She was a self-centered young woman who would have aged into an antisocial old woman. She wouldn't have killed anyone, including herself, except to benefit Rosie Hoffsteder.'

'You know, Mrs. Q., I didn't give you enough credit for smarts when I was in your class. I don't think anyone did. You do have one small thing wrong, though. Lisa never asked for money. She wanted Heidi back. All of a sudden, the little mother wanted nothing except her sweet, sweet babe. Three bloody years later. Can you believe it?'

I was, I must admit, having difficulty believing it, perhaps because I found it difficult to believe Lisa never demanded money.

Jerry Joe picked up the rolling pin he'd laid on the table top between us and began rolling an imaginary pie crust on the bare wood. 'She was afraid to ask the social services people for help. They might take Heidi away from her forever because of the way she'd dumped the kid in the first place.'

'Jerry Joe, there must be a reason that Lisa needed her daughter back right now, and at gunpoint.' I said this the way I used to say, 'Jerry Joe, there must be a reason that you never have your English assignment in on time.'

He gave me the old, familiar, slyly embarrassed look. 'It's because she finally got all of her memory back. From the coma? I guess it takes a while sometimes for all the little details to resurface.'

This felt like the point of no return. This was where I wanted to have the boiling water, the Smith and Wesson, the Paul McMorris handy. I thought of Julian tooling along a southern highway, his troops singing *Love Me Tender* or *Blue Suede Shoes*, while in my cozy kitchen Jerry Joe Hoffsteder teetered on the brink of saying something that would change matters — change me — forever.

But — 'Go on,' I had to say.

He continued to knead my table with the rolling pin. 'What she remembered was — the night she took Heidi to John, I was there, too. She remembered changing her mind at the last moment, putting Heidi back into the car, the arguing between her and me. She remembered that I insisted on driving.'

He shoved the rolling pin, letting go, and it rotated itself off the edge of the table to clatter-smack the linoleum.

'I was so mad,' he said, looking me in the eyes, 'I aimed the Bronco at the ditch.'

At last, my kettle began to rattle and hiss. I stood up automatically, took down two cups, and spooned them with instant coffee. I doubted I could disable Jerry Joe with boiling water or coffee. I'd only end up scalding myself and making him madder than he already was — in both meanings of the word. His horror the mayor — a horror indeed. No wonder the poor woman was desperate to rescue her daughter from the range of a father willing to mutilate them and himself in a moment's rage.

'It seemed like a good idea not to tell the world I was with Lisa in the car,' he was saying. 'Especially since my injuries were only a few bruises. John hid me in the house till all the excitement calmed down, and then Darrell drove me back to Preble City.'

I set one cup in front of him and sat down with mine. 'And Mickey Faust. Did he know Lisa or Rosie or you or anything about this mess?'

Jerry Joe batted at the question with a lethargic hand and said nothing.

'Well? Was he — what? — a bystander who happened to see too much?' I persisted.

'I don't know if he saw a damn thing, tell you the truth. He *might* have.'

Here was another horror — murder as a precautionary measure.

'You don't care that your parents think their Rosie murdered two people over a sexual disagreement?'

He shrugged. 'You want them to think their Jerry Joe murdered three people, one of them his own flesh and blood?'

This was perhaps the most horrible of

all — that his sister hadn't been properly mourned as yet because no one besides me knew. I needed to stay alive for her sake, if not my own — to set the record straight.

'You still think I'm a bad guy? Have I said one thing that amounts to a confession to murder? No. And I won't. But your trouble is, Tirzzy, you're too stubborn to admit you were wrong about me. You'll keep prying and pestering, and I don't have time for that.' He sipped at the coffee. 'Another thing. Would I have come here this afternoon to commit murder? Let all the neighbors see me? Let you tell Paul on the phone about me? Everyone knows I'm here having a nice, quiet supper with you. I'd be crazy to hurt you, wouldn't I?'

The word 'crazy' brought my backbone to attention. I blew on my coffee, wondering if he would let me simply walk out my back door and over to Velma's. Casually, I turned my head that direction and confirmed that there were no lights in the windows, or other sign of her return.

'The thing is, an elderly lady like you is

prone to falls. So, say I was to ask you for some homemade relish or something, to pad out our meal, and say you went to get it and slipped on the cellar stairs.' He put the flat of one hand on the table top and groped under the table with the other, bringing up the rolling pin. 'I'd try to revive you before calling the professionals, but you took one whale of a blow to your head.'

We stared one another in the eyes; Jerry Joe's were full of deserts of vast eternity. Being right about Lisa's murderer provided me about as much personal pleasure as sticking my finger in a socket to prove it would shock.

Never again would I waste an afternoon playing solitaire. Tomorrow, if I were physically able, I'd resurrect the Your Own Write books from my lingerie drawer, and I'd write, write, write. Why should I fear the ridicule of friends? Which of my friends could write any better?

Our tableau held until the unmistakable chunk of a closing car door carried in on the evening air. I gasped a too-quick breath and choked on it. Paul, after all? Velma?

Before I could twist around to check, Jerry Joe said, 'Keep quiet. You shout for anyone to come in here, they're bound to suffer a fall too, trying to grab and save you.'

'How did you make Rosie write a suicide note?'

'If the police were to study it more carefully, maybe they'd decide she didn't.'

'Why did you take my Smith and Wesson after shooting Mickey Foust with Lisa's Smith and Wesson?'

'I'm not saying that I did, but if I did? Maybe the kid drew it on me — tried to — and I twisted it out of his hand and stuck it in my pocket while we talked. I could have forgotten I had it till, oh say, I was halfway to my car parked three blocks away. And then I might have hid it in my house, in case I needed to shoot someone again someday. Maybe.' He laughed a sharp, short laugh. 'And maybe I was astonished when I got a good gander at it, too — at how much it looked like the other gun. If I'd had another gun, you understand.'

He gave me a smart-alecky wink.

'If you're going to murder me, I want to hear you admit it in plain English, Jerry Joe Hoffsteder.' I showed him the sternest look I could muster, a cold you-straighten-up-right-this-minute stare.

With folded forearms on the table, he leaned at me. He opened his mouth, his eyes shifted to my left, and he sang out heartily, 'Mrs. Newby. I think it's Mrs. Newby. Is that you or your younger sister?'

She stood peering through the screen at us, backlighted by the last throes of sunlight.

'Velma!' I put my hand out at her like a policeman stopping traffic, except mine shook like the dickens. 'Don't come in here. I mean, Jerry Joe and I have things to discuss.'

'Oh. All right. I just had something to show you.'

'Not now,' I said, and was drowned out by Jerry Joe's booming, 'Don't let me stop you. I'll just warm up the Chinese peace offering I brought for Mrs. Quizenberry's supper, while you ladies talk.'

'We don't have anything to talk about,'

I said. 'We had a disagreement over a dog, and we aren't speaking to each other.'

'No, Tirzzy,' Velma piped up. 'That's what I wanted to show you. I got a new dog. Fifi.'

Now I saw the line of a leash leading from her arm to my porch floor, and the silhouetted mound of an animal at the end. I shut my eyes briefly, thankful to know, in possibly my last few minutes, that Velma had forgiven me.

'Bring the pup inside,' Jerry Joe invited. Although he rose to his feet, the polite gesture was nullified by his also whipping my rolling pin up out of sight behind his back.

'No! I forbid it! I don't want a dirty, dumb dog in my house!' I think I was wringing my hands. 'In fact, I don't want you in my house either. I never liked you and I never liked Yappy.' My voice wobbled up the scale toward very high C.

As Velma hesitated, I picked up the first thing at hand — my almost-full cup — and lobbed it at the screen. Coffee flew every which way, including through the screenwire, making Velma jump aside. Behind me, Jerry Joe chuckled and sidled along the table. I sidled the other direction, but whereas he was silent and sure, I bumped into chairs in a clumsy stagger.

'Damn it, Velma, go home.'

'I'm disappointed in you, Tirzah,' Velma said, frowning at me through the dripping screen. 'Hysterical to the point of rude. Not you at all. You need professional help.'

With that, she bent to undo the leash, yanked open the door, and said in a high, firm voice, 'Sic him.'

The dog grew. The motionless little shape rose up and became a large blur of motion. Fifi burst through the doorway, toenails scrabbling for purchase on the smooth floor, and hurtled across the short space to Jerry Joe, who, as surprised as I, thought too late of taking evasive action. Launching herself high as his throat, she locked jaws on his defending arm and hauled it down as she fell. Backing away, growling, she worried the arm — and undoubtedly Jerry Joe. He swung the rolling pin around and struck at her head, but Fifi, apparently expecting something of the sort, deflected it with a neat side sling of her body that carried Jerry Joe around with her, putting his back to the table. When he raised the rolling pin for a second try, I reached across and snatched it out of his hand.

'The more you fight, the worse you'll get hurt,' Velma shouted at Jerry Joe. 'Sit down and hold still, and I'll call her off.'

If I ever have to credit Jerry Joe Hoffsteder with one admirable moment, it will be that one, when his willpower overcame his instinct, and he stopped fighting the dog. After he managed to fall into his chair, Velma, true to her word, ordered Fifi to sit too.

The dog — mostly German shepherd, I could see now — backed into an alert, seated pose two feet from Jerry Joe's shoes, her tongue lolling out and her tail beating a happy tattoo.

'Good God, Velma,' I said, my legs as graceless as two logs as I stumbled to the telephone to dial 911. 'Whatever possessed you to get such a ferocious dog?'

'I went in to the pound to get another

lap dog, but then I saw this one they were going to destroy.'

Jerry Joe clutched his wounded arm, eyes glazed, obviously trying to move no muscle.

'She'd been trained to be an attack dog but she failed the final exams,' Velma continued. 'Fifi pees at loud noises. I'm sorry about your porch when you threw the cup. And she gets car sick. So she's not exactly the sidekick any policeman wants. But I thought that with you for a neighbor, a Jekyll and Hyde canine would be the perfect pet for me.'

'Police department,' a male voice said in my ear.

I announced my name, address, and birth date before he could ask. Next I told him I'd made a senior citizen's arrest on a man responsible for killing three people, who'd had his heart set on making it four or five. I suggested they send a patrol car right away, before our watchdog had to urinate or throw up.

I didn't ask for Paul McMorris. I guess I didn't need him.

17

Since I didn't have to go to the county courthouse the next day after all, Paul and I had supper at Hake's a night earlier than we'd planned. He brought me a white rose corsage of apology or celebration, or because Kroger's was having a sale.

'How did Velma know?' he asked when we were halfway through our shrimp scampi. 'That you needed help, I mean.'

'She didn't. She was coming over to show me her new dog. But seeing Jerry Joe made her uneasy, knowing how I felt about him. She could see I was upset about something. And then I was extremely rude to her. I have my faults, she says, but rudeness isn't one of them. Velma has her faults, but slow-wittedness isn't one of them.'.

'Unlike present company.' Paul grinned and shook his head. 'Radishes, indeed.'

He wouldn't have thought it funny if

he'd been the one belching for help.

I glanced around the walnut and flocked-wallpaper room, its tables swathed in white tablecloths gleaming with silverware and crystal goblets. At another table, a woman laughed a husky German-sounding laugh, and further off a swinging door whispered someone in or out. The scents of garlic and coffee hung in the air like invisible fog. The crisp peach-colored napkin in my lap, the pistol-gripped knife that I lifted to stroke ivory butter on my golden roll — everything seemed wondrous.

'What will happen to Heidi?' I asked later, as we drove home. The star-spangled night was as beautiful as Hake's had been, except it smelled of skunk and manure.

'If John Junior can prove he had nothing to do with the murders, there's a good chance he'll be allowed to keep Heidi. He's her uncle, after all.'

If anyone in that family is fit to raise a child, it's John Junior. Did Jerry Joe say how he got the idea to frame Rosie?'

'She apparently saw his car in the neighborhood the day that Mickey was shot, and she asked Jerry Joe if he'd noticed anything that would clear her of suspicion. It occurred to him that he could do just the opposite.'

'And I suppose he'll get off on an insanity plea.'

'It's unlikely. The defense would have to prove Jerry Joe was incapable of distinguishing right from wrong and that he simply wasn't able to control himself. Pretty hard to claim and prove. But even if he did get a not guilty by reason of insanity verdict, his punishment would certainly not be easy for him — incarceration in a home for the criminally insane, away from all his creature comforts. While someone else runs for governor.' After a moment's silence, Paul chuckled. 'We need a new mayor. You ought to run.'

'Oh, I will, as far from Preble City as possible, if anyone else suggests it.'

Silence settled over us like a comfortable quilt.

I tipped back my seat and pretended to sleep, or maybe it was genuine. I drifted in that in-between state where every thought seems profound and all truths become self-evident.

Paul and I would be friends — perhaps more than friends — but he would never ask me to marry him, and if he did, I'd turn down the opportunity. We'd each been on our own too long. I wouldn't want to live in his house, he wouldn't want to live in mine, and that's only the beginning of the civilized sacrifices and compromises that married people must make.

I smiled as I pictured Paul dodging the matrimonial clutches of Bea Adair and some of my other widowed friends. I myself had better things to do than to chase after men — innocent ones, anyway.

For starters — no more shillyshallying — I'd write a novel.